NEW YORK REVIEW BOOKS
CLASSICS

T0021922

IN THE CAFÉ OF LOST YOUTH

PATRICK MODIANO was born in the Boulogne-Billancourt suburb of Paris near the end of the Nazi occupation of France. He studied at the Lycée Henri-IV and the Sorbonne. As a teenager he took geometry lessons with the writer Raymond Queneau, who would play a key role in his development. He has written more than thirty works of fiction, including novels, children's books, and the screenplay for Louis Malle's film *Lacombe, Lucien*. In 2014, Modiano won the Nobel Prize in Literature.

CHRIS CLARKE was born and raised in British Columbia, Canada, and lives and works in and around New York City. His published translations include work by Oulipo members Raymond Queneau and Olivier Salon. He currently teaches French and is translating a novel by Pierre Mac Orlan, which will be published in 2016.

IN THE CAFÉ OF
LOST YOUTH

PATRICK MODIANO

Translated from the French by
CHRIS CLARKE

NEW YORK REVIEW BOOKS

New York

THIS IS A NEW YORK REVIEW BOOK
PUBLISHED BY THE NEW YORK REVIEW OF BOOKS
435 Hudson Street, New York, NY 10014
www.nyrb.com

Originally published in French as *Dans le café de la jeunesse perdue*.

Library of Congress Cataloging-in-Publication Data
Names: Modiano, Patrick, 1945– author. | Clarke, Chris (Translator) translator.
Title: In the cafe of lost youth / Patrick Modiano ; translated by Chris Clarke.
Other titles: Dans le cafe de la jeunesse perdue. English
Description: New York : New York Review Books, 2016. | Series: New York
  Review Books Classics
Identifiers: LCCN 2015039566 | ISBN 9781590179536 (paperback)
Subjects: | BISAC: FICTION / Psychological. | FICTION / Historical. |
  FICTION / Literary.
Classification: LCC PQ2673.O3 D3613 2016 | DDC 843/.914—dc23
LC record available at http://lccn.loc.gov/2015039566

ISBN 978-1-59017-953-6
Available as an electronic book; ISBN 978-1-59017-954-3

Printed in the United States of America on acid-free paper.
10 9 8 7 6

At the halfway point of the journey making up real life, we were surrounded by a gloomy melancholy, one expressed by so very many derisive and sorrowful words in the café of the lost youth.

—Guy Debord

THERE were two entrances to the café, but she always opted for the narrower one hidden in the shadows. She always chose the same table at the back of the little room. At first she didn't speak to anyone, then she got to know the regulars of the Condé, most of whom were about our age, I'd say between nineteen and twenty-five years old. She sometimes sat at their tables, but most of the time she was faithful to her spot, way at the back.

She wasn't regular about her visits. You might find her sitting there very early in the morning. Or sometimes she appeared around midnight and stayed until closing time. Along with Le Bouquet and La Pergola, it was one of the cafés in the neighborhood that closed the latest, and the one with the strangest clientele. I often ask myself, now that time has passed, if it wasn't her presence alone that gave this place and these people their strangeness, as if she had impregnated them all with her scent.

Suppose that you were blindfolded, led there, and seated at a table, then your blindfold was removed and you were given a few minutes to answer the question: What part of Paris are you in? You only would have had to observe your neighbors and listen to their comments, and you might have been able to guess: Somewhere not far from the Carrefour de l'Odéon, which in my mind I always picture looking dreary in the rain.

One day a photographer had come into the Condé. Nothing about his appearance distinguished him from the customers. The same age, the same sloppy style of dress. He wore a jacket that was too long, cotton pants, and big army-issue shoes. He took a number of photos of the people who frequented the Condé. He became a regular himself and, as far as the others were concerned, it was as if he was taking family photos. Quite some time later, they appeared in a monograph about Paris, with only the customers' first names or nicknames as captions. And she appears in several of these photographs. She caught the light better than the others, as they say in the film business. Of them all, she's the one you notice first. At the bottom of the page, in the captions, she's referred to as "Louki." "From left to right: Zacharias, Louki, Tarzan, Jean-Michel, Fred, and Ali Cherif." "Foreground, seated at the bar: Louki. Behind her: Annet, Don Carlos, Mireille, Adamov, and Dr. Vala." She has good posture, whereas the others slouch; the one named Fred, for example, has fallen asleep with his head against the imitation-leather banquette and hasn't shaved in several days. Needless to say, the name Louki was given to her once she became a regular at the Condé. I was there one night when she came in towards midnight and only Tarzan, Fred, Zacharias, and Mireille were left, all sitting at the same table. It was Tarzan who shouted, "Look, here comes Louki." She appeared frightened at first, then she smiled. Zacharias got up and, with a tone of feigned solemnity, proclaimed, "Tonight, I baptize thee. Henceforth, you shall be called Louki." And as the hours went by and they all referred to her as Louki, I really think she felt relieved to have this new name. Yes, relieved. Actually, the more I think about it, the more I end up with the same impression I had at first: She was taking refuge here, at the Condé, as if she were running from something, trying to escape some danger. This thought came to me upon seeing her alone, all the way at the back where no one would notice her. And even when she mingled with the others, she didn't draw attention to herself. She remained quiet and reserved, and seemed happy just to listen. I had even thought that she chose the noisy groups, the loudmouths, to feel safer, otherwise she wouldn't have been likely to spend all her time seated at a table with Zacharias, Jean-Michel, Fred, Tarzan, and La Houpa. With them, she could blend into the background and was no more than an anonymous extra, one of the people referred to in the photo captions as "unidentified person" or, more simply, "X." Yes, at first, at the Condé, I never saw her have a one-on-one discussion with anyone. What's more, there was no drawback to one of the loudmouths calling her Louki because it wasn't really her name.

And yet, if you watched her carefully, you would notice certain details that set her apart from the others. She took a great deal of care with her clothing, which was unusual among the patrons of the Condé. She lit a cigarette one evening as she sat with Tarzan, Ali Cherif, and La Houpa, and I was struck by the slenderness of her hands. And above all, her nails shone. They were painted with a clear varnish. This detail may seem a bit trivial, so let's stick to what's important. First of all, some details about the Condé's regulars are necessary. Well, they were between nineteen and twenty-five years old, with the exception of a few customers such as Babilée, Adamov, and Dr. Vala who were approaching fifty, but no one paid any mind to their ages. Babilée,

Adamov, and Dr. Vala still clung to their youthfulness, men we might describe with the melodious and obsolete moniker "bohemians." When I look up "bohemian" in the dictionary, I find: A person who leads a wandering life, without rules or worries about the next day. Truly a definition well suited to those who frequented the Condé. Some, like Tarzan, Jean-Michel, and Fred, claimed to have had numerous run-ins with the police since their adolescence, and La Houpa had escaped from the Bon Pasteur Correctional Facility at sixteen. But we were on the Rive Gauche and most of them lived in the sheltered world of literature and the arts. I myself was going to school. I didn't dare tell this to them, and I didn't often mingle with their group.

I'd really felt that she was different from the others. Where had she come from before we had given her a new name? Often, the regulars of the Condé had books with them that they would set down nonchalantly on the table before them, the covers stained with wine. *The Songs of Maldoror. Illuminations. The Mysterious Barricades.* But Louki, at least at first, was always empty-handed. Later, she must have wanted to be like the others, and one day at the Condé I came upon her alone, reading. After that, she was never without her book. She kept it out somewhere noticeable on the table whenever she ended up with Adamov and the others, and it was as if this book were her passport or a residence permit that legitimized her presence by their sides. But nobody paid it any mind, not Adamov, not Babilée, not Tarzan, not La Houpa. It was a pocket book with a soiled cover like one you'd buy used along the quay; its title had been printed in large red letters. A French translation of *Lost Horizon*. At the time, it meant nothing to me. I should have asked her what the book was about, but I had foolishly told myself that *Lost Horizon* was nothing but an accessory for her, assuming she pretended to read it in order to fall in step with the customers of the Condé. If someone passing by was to shoot a furtive glance inside—maybe going so far as to press his forehead against the window for a moment—he might have taken the patrons for a typical student clientele. But he would have changed his mind if he noticed the quantity of alcohol they were consuming at Tarzan, Mireille, Fred, and La Houpa's table. In the peaceful cafés of the Latin Quarter, they never would drink like that. Sure, during the slack hours of the afternoon, the Condé could pass for one of them. But once the day started to draw to a close, it became the meeting place of what a romantic philosopher once called "the Lost Youth." Why this café instead of another? Because of the owner, Madame Chadly, who never seemed surprised by anything and demonstrated a certain indulgence toward her customers. Many years later, the streets of the neighborhood no longer offering anything but the windows of luxury boutiques, the site of the Condé since replaced by a leather shop, I ran into Madame Chadly on the other bank of the Seine, on the way up rue Blanche. She didn't recognize me right away. We walked a while, side by side, talking about the Condé. Her husband, an Algerian, had purchased the business after the war. She remembered all of our names. She often wondered what had become of us, although she had no illusions. She had known right from the outset that things would turn out badly for us. Stray dogs, she told me. And as we bade each other farewell in front of the pharmacy at place Blanche, she confided to me, looking me right in the eye: "Louki was my favorite."

When Louki was sitting with Tarzan, Fred, and La

Houpa, did she drink as much as they did, or did she pretend so as to not upset them? In any case, her back straight, her movements slow and gracious, her smile almost imperceptible, she held her liquor extremely well. At the bar, it's easier to cheat. You wait for a moment when your friends aren't paying attention and you empty your glass into the sink. But there, at one of the tables of the Condé, it was more difficult. The others forced you to keep up with their drinking escapades. On that subject, they revealed themselves to be extremely touchy and considered you unworthy of their group if you didn't accompany them to the very end of what they referred to as their "journeys." As for other kinds of intoxicants, I had suspected without being certain that Louki used some, with certain members of the group. All the same, nothing in her eyes or her attitude would lead you to believe that she escaped to synthetic paradises.

I've often wondered if an acquaintance had told her about the Condé before she went in for the first time. Or if someone had asked her to meet him in the café and then not turned up. If so, she might have sat there at her table, day after day and night after night, hoping to run into him once again in this place that was the sole point linking her to this unknown person. No other way of getting in touch with him. No address. No phone number. Just a first name. And yet, maybe she had just washed up there by chance, as I had. She was in the neighborhood and had sought shelter from the rain. I've always believed that certain places are like magnets and draw you towards them should you happen to walk within their radius. And this occurs imperceptibly, without you even suspecting. All it takes is a sloping street, a sunny sidewalk, or maybe a shady one. Or perhaps a downpour. And this leads you straight there, to the exact spot you're meant to wash up. It seems to me that because of its location, the Condé had that sort of magnetic power, and if one were to calculate the probability, the results would indicate that within a fairly large area, it was inevitable that you would drift towards it. This much I know from personal experience.

One of the members of the group, Bowing, the one we called "the Captain," had undertaken a venture of which the others approved. For going on three years he had been taking note of the names of the Condé's customers as they arrived, in each instance jotting down the date and exact time. He had charged two of his friends with the responsibility of performing the same task at Le Bouquet and La Pergola, both of which stayed open all night. Unfortunately, in both of those cafés, the customers didn't always want to give their names. It was as if Bowing were trying to save butterflies that fluttered around a lamp from being forgotten. He envisioned a great register where the names of the customers of all the cafés of Paris were recorded, with notes made of their successive arrivals and departures. He was haunted by what he called "fixed points."

In this uninterrupted stream of women, men, children, and dogs that pass by and end up lost from sight among the streets, it would be nice to hold on to a face once in a while. Yes, according to Bowing, amidst the maelstrom that is a large city, you had to find a few fixed points. Before he left to go abroad, he gave me the notebook where, day after day for three years, the customers of the Condé had been listed. Louki only appeared under her borrowed name, and she is mentioned for the first time one January 23rd. The winter that year had been particularly severe, and some of us didn't leave the Condé all day so as to stay out of the cold. The

Captain also made note of our addresses in order to make it possible to imagine the customary route that each of us took to the Condé. For Bowing, it was another way of establishing fixed points. He doesn't mention her address right away. It's not until March 18th that you read, "2 p.m. Louki, 16, rue Fermat, 14th arrondissement." But on September 5th of that same year, she had moved: "11:40 p.m. Louki, 8, rue Cels, 14th arrondissement." I assume that Bowing drew our routes to the Condé on large maps of Paris and that for this task, the Captain would use ballpoint pens with different-colored ink. Maybe he wanted to know if it was possible for us to run into each other before we even reached our destination.

As a matter of fact, I remember having met Louki one day in an unfamiliar neighborhood after paying a visit to a distant cousin of my parents'. When I left his place, I was walking towards the Porte Maillot Métro, and we ran into each other at the far end of avenue de la Grande-Armée. I stared at her and she gave me an anxious look, as if I had caught her in the middle of an embarrassing situation. I held out my hand to her. "We've seen each other at the Condé," I told her, and the café had suddenly seemed as if it were on the other side of the world. She gave a little embarrassed smile: "Oh, sure, at the Condé." It wasn't too long after she had first appeared there. She hadn't yet started to mingle with the others and Zacharias hadn't yet named her Louki. "The Condé's a funny little café, huh?" She had given a nod of her head in agreement. We walked a short ways together, and she told me that she lived nearby, but added that she wasn't at all fond of the neighborhood. It's stupid, I could have found out her real name that day. Then we went our separate ways at the Porte Maillot, by the entrance to the Métro, and I watched her recede into the distance towards Neuilly and the Bois de Boulogne, walking more and more slowly, as if to give someone the opportunity to catch up to her. I got a feeling that she wouldn't come back to the Condé and that would be the last I heard of her. She would disappear into what Bowing called "the anonymity of the big city," which he endeavored to combat by filling the pages of his notebook with names. A 190-page Clairefontaine notebook with a plastic-coated red cover. To be frank, that doesn't amount to much. If you flip through the notebook, other than fleeting names and addresses, there is little to be learned about either these people or me. Doubtless the Captain figured it was already quite significant to have named us and "fixed" us somewhere. As for the rest... At the Condé, we never questioned each other about our origins. We were too young and we didn't even have pasts to reveal, we lived in the present. Even the older customers like Adamov, Babilée, or Dr. Vala never alluded to their pasts. They were just happy to be there, among us. It isn't until now, after all this time, that I feel regret; I would have liked for him to have been more precise in his notebook, and for him to have included a short biography of each of them. Did he really believe that a name and an address would later be enough to keep track of a life? And especially when the names weren't real? "Louki. Monday, February 12th, 11 p.m." "Louki. April 28th, 2 p.m." He also indicated the seats they took around the tables each day. Sometimes there weren't even names. Three times in June of that year, he noted: "Louki with the brown-haired guy in the suede jacket." He hadn't asked him his name, this fellow, or else he had been refused an answer. Apparently the guy wasn't a regular customer. The brown-haired guy in the suede jacket had been lost forever among the streets of Paris, and Bowing had only managed to fix his shadow for a few seconds. Also, there were inaccuracies in his notebook. I established points of reference which corroborate my belief that she had not in fact come to the Condé for the first time in January, as Bowing would have you believe. I have a memory of her from well before that date. The Captain didn't mention her before the others started to call her Louki, and I guess that until then he hadn't noticed her presence. She hadn't even been given a vague entry along the lines of "2 p.m. A brunette with green eyes," something similar to "the brown-haired guy in the suede jacket."

She first turned up in October of the previous year. I found a reference point in the Captain's notebook. "October 15th, 9 p.m. Zacharias's birthday. At his table, Annet, Don Carlos, Mireille, La Houpa, Fred, Adamov." I can remember it perfectly. She was at their table. Why didn't Bowing have the curiosity to ask her name? The accounts are fragile and contradictory, but I am certain of her presence that evening. Everything that made her invisible to Bowing's gaze had struck me. Her timidity, her languid movements, her smile, and above all her silence. She had been next to Adamov. Perhaps it was because of him that she had come to the Condé. I had often run into Adamov around Odéon, as well as further up around Saint-Julien-le-Pauvre. Each time, he was walking with his hand resting on the shoulder of a young girl. A blind man allowing himself to be guided. And yet he looked as if he was observing everything with that tragic, doglike stare. And each time, it seemed to me, it was a different young girl serving as his guide. Or nurse. Why not her? Well, as it turned out, she left the Condé with Adamov that night. I saw them head down the empty street towards Odéon, Adamov with his hand on her shoulder, advancing with his methodical gait. You might have thought she was afraid of going too fast, and sometimes she would stop a moment, as if to allow him to catch his breath. At the Carrefour de l'Odéon, Adamov shook her hand somewhat solemnly, then she rushed into the mouth of the Métro. He resumed his somnambulist's stride, straight on towards Saint-André-des-Arts. And her? Yes, she had begun to frequent the Condé that same autumn. And that's definitely not a coincidence. For me, autumn has never been a sad season. The dying leaves and the days that grow shorter and shorter have never evoked the end of something for me but instead brought with them anticipation for the future. In Paris, during these October evenings, there is an electricity in the air at dusk. Even when it rains. I don't feel down at that time of night, nor does it seem that time is passing too swiftly. I have the feeling that anything is possible. The year begins in the month of October. That's when classes start again and to me it's the season to take on new projects. So if she came to the Condé in October, it's because she had broken ties with some entire part of her life and she wanted to do what they refer to in novels as "turning over a new leaf." Moreover, a clue proves to me that I'm not mistaken. At the Condé, she was given a new name. Zacharias, that day, had even spoken of baptism. It was in some way a second birth.

As for the brown-haired guy in the suede jacket, unfortunately he doesn't appear in the photos taken at the Condé. Too bad. People often end up being identified thanks to a photo. It gets published in a newspaper asking witnesses to come forward. Was he a member of the group, one whose name Bowing didn't know and was too lazy to ask?

Last evening, I carefully went through every page in the notebook. "Louki with the brown-haired guy in the suede jacket." And to my great surprise, I noticed that it wasn't only in June that the Captain mentioned this stranger. At the bottom of one page, he had hurriedly scrawled, "May 24th. Louki with the brown-haired guy in the suede jacket." And the same caption is found again, twice more, in April. I had asked Bowing why every time she was mentioned, he had underlined her name in blue pencil, as if to make her stand out from the others. No, he wasn't the one who had done that. One day he had been sitting at the bar, jotting down the customers present in his notebook, when a man standing beside him had interrupted his work. A guy in his forties who knew Dr. Vala. He spoke softly and smoked American cigarettes. Bowing had felt trusting and had said a few words to him about what he called his Golden Book. The other man had seemed interested. He was an "art publisher." Sure, he knew the fellow who had taken photos at the Condé some time ago. He intended to publish them in a book that would be titled *A Café in Paris*. Would Bowing be kind enough to lend him his notebook until the next day, as it might help him in selecting captions for the photos? The following day, he had returned the notebook and had never been seen at the Condé again. The Captain had been surprised to notice that each occurrence of the name Louki had been underlined in blue pencil. He had wanted to know more about it and had asked Dr. Vala a few questions about the art publisher. Vala had been surprised. "Ah, he told you he published art books, did he?" He knew him only in passing, from having run into him regularly at La Malène on rue Saint-Benoît as well as at the Montana, where he had even played dice with him a few times. The fellow had been around the neighborhood for a long time. His name? Caisley. Vala seemed a little embarrassed to speak of him. And when Bowing had alluded to the blue pencil marks beneath the name Louki, a worried expression had crossed the doctor's face. It had been quite fleeting. And then he had smiled. "He must be interested in the little one. She's so pretty. But what a strange idea to fill your notebook with all of those names. I find you all quite amusing, you and your friends and your pataphysical experiments." He mixed them up—pataphysics, lettrism, automatic writing, metagraphics, and all of the experiments that interested the Condé's more literary patrons, like Bowing, Jean-Michel, Fred, Babilée, Larronde, or Adamov. "What's more, it's dangerous to do that," Dr. Vala had added with a serious tone. "Your notebook, it's almost like a police register or a precinct logbook. It's as if we had all been taken in a raid."

Bowing had objected, trying to explain his theory of fixed points, but from that day on the Captain had the impression that Dr. Vala distrusted him and even wanted to avoid him.

This Caisley hadn't just underlined the name Louki. Each time there was a mention of "the brown-haired guy in the suede jacket" in the notebook there were two blue pencil lines. All of this troubled Bowing quite a bit, and for the next few days he had roamed around rue Saint-Benoît with hopes of running into this so-called art publisher, perhaps at La Malène or the Montana, to ask him to explain himself. He never found him. Some time later, Bowing ended up leaving France and gave me the notebook, as if he had wanted me to take over his research. But it's too late now. And if this whole period still endures in my memory, it's because of questions that have remained unanswered.

Sometimes during the quieter moments of the day, on the way home from the office, and often in the solitude of Sunday evenings, a detail comes back to me. With the utmost concentration, I try to gather others like it and make note of them on the remaining blank pages at the back of Bowing's notebook. I too have gone hunting for fixed points. It's just a hobby, not unlike how others do crosswords or play solitaire. The names and the dates in Bowing's notebook help me quite a lot, every now and then they remind me of some particular detail, some rainy day or sunny afternoon. I've always been very sensitive to the seasons. One evening, Louki came into the Condé, her hair soaking wet either from a downpour or rather one of those interminable rains that we get in November or the beginning of spring. Madame Chadly was behind the bar that day. She went up to the second floor, to her tiny apartment, and fetched a bath towel. As the notebook tells us, that night Zacharias, Annet, Don Carlos, Mireille, La Houpa, Fred, and Maurice Raphaël were all gathered at one table. Zacharias took the towel and dried Louki's hair with it before knotting it around her head like a turban. She sat down at their table, they made her drink a hot toddy, and she stayed quite late with them, the turban on her head. On the way out of the Condé, around two in the morning, it was still raining. We were all standing in the doorway and Louki was still wearing her turban. Madame Chadly had turned off the café lights and gone up to bed. She opened her mezzanine window and suggested that we go up to her place to take shelter. But Maurice Raphaël gallantly told her: "Don't worry yourself about it, madame. It is time we let you sleep." He was a handsome, dark-haired man, older than us, a regular customer at the Condé whom Zacharias referred to as "the Jaguar" because of the way he walked and his cat-like mannerisms. Like Adamov and Larronde, he had published several books, but he never spoke of them to us. There was mystery surrounding him, and we even thought he may have had ties to the underworld. The rain had redoubled its efforts, a real monsoon, but it wasn't a big deal for the others since they lived in the vicinity. Soon only Louki, Maurice Raphaël, and I remained under the porch. "Would you both like a ride back home?" offered Maurice Raphaël. We ran through the rain to the bottom of the street where he had parked his car, an old black Ford. Louki sat next to him, and I sat in the backseat. "Who am I dropping off first?" said Maurice Raphaël. Louki gave him her address, adding that it was up from Montparnasse Cemetery. "So you live in Limbo," he said. And I think that neither she nor I understood what he meant by "Limbo." I asked him to drop me off a little way past the gates of the Luxembourg, on the corner of Val-de-Grâce. I didn't want him to know exactly where I lived for fear that he might ask questions.

I shook hands with Louki and then with Maurice Raphaël, realizing that neither of them knew my name. I was a very unassuming customer at the Condé and I kept my distance, happy just to listen to them all. And that was plenty for me. I felt good around them. For me, the Condé was a refuge from all the drabness I anticipated in life. There will one day be a part of me—the best part—that I will be forced to leave behind there.

"A smart decision, living in Val-de-Grâce," Maurice Raphaël said to me.

He was smiling at me and his smile seemed to express both kindness and irony.

"See you soon," Louki said.

I climbed out of the car, and before I turned back, I waited for it to disappear over by Port-Royal. Truth be told, I didn't actually live in Val-de-Grâce, but a bit farther down in a building at 85, boulevard Saint-Michel, where I had miraculously found a room when I first arrived in Paris. From the window, I could see the dark façade of my school. That night, I couldn't tear my eyes away from that monumental façade or from the great stone stairs of the entrance. What would they think if they found out I took those steps almost every day and was a student at the École Supérieure des Mines? Did Zacharias, La Houpa, Ali Cherif, or Don Carlos really know what the École des Mines was all about? It was necessary for me to keep this a secret or I risked them poking fun at me or distrusting me. What did the École des Mines represent to Adamov, Larronde, or Maurice Raphaël? Nothing, of course. They would suggest I stop going to such a place. If I spent a lot of time at the Condé, it was because I wanted them to give me such advice, once and for all. Louki and Maurice Raphaël would have already made it to the other side of Montparnasse Cemetery, over to the area that he called Limbo. And I remained, standing there in the dark, up against my window, contemplating that darkened façade. It could have passed for the abandoned train station of a provincial town. On the walls of the neighboring building, I had noticed bullet holes, like they had shot someone there. I quietly repeated those four words that seemed more and more foreign, "École Supérieure des Mines."

I was fortunate that particular young man was sitting next to me at the Condé and we struck up such a comfortable conversation. It was the first time I had been in that establishment, and I was old enough to be his father. The notebook in which he'd kept track of the Condé's customers, day in and day out for the past three years, made my work easier. I feel bad for hiding the true reason I wanted to consult his document but I simply did so in hopes that he would be kind enough to lend it to me. And was I lying when I told him I was an art publisher?

I was pretty certain that he believed me. That's the advantage of being twenty years older than someone: They don't know your past. And even if they ask you a couple of distracted questions about what your life has been up until that point, you can make it up completely. A new life. They're not going to go and check. As you tell of this imaginary life, great breaths of fresh air rush across a closed room in which you have been unable to breathe for a long time. A window abruptly opens, the shutters bang in the breeze. You have, once again, a future before you.

An art publisher. It came to me without even thinking. If I had been asked what I was going to be when I was older, some twenty years ago, I would have mumbled: an art publisher. And well, today I said it. Nothing has changed. All of those years are done and gone.

Except I haven't quite wiped clean the slate of the past. There are still some witnesses, a few survivors among those who had been our contemporaries. One evening, at the Montana, I asked Dr. Vala when he was born. We were born the same year. And I reminded him that we had met in the olden days, in that very bar, when the area still shone as brightly as it once had. And moreover, it seemed to me that I had run into him well before, elsewhere in Paris, on the Rive Droite. I was even certain of it. Dryly, Vala had ordered a bottle of Vittel, cutting me off at the very moment it seemed as if I might bring up unpleasant memories. I shut up. We live at the mercy of certain silences. We have all known things about each other for a long time. So we try to avoid each other. It would be for the best, of course, if none of us were ever to see each other again.

What a strange coincidence … I came across Vala the very first afternoon I went into the Condé. He was sitting at a table at the back with two or three young people. He shot me the alarmed look of a bon vivant who finds himself in the presence of a ghost. I gave him a smile. I shook his hand without saying a thing. I felt that the least word on my part risked making him uncomfortable in front of his new friends. He seemed relieved by my silence and discretion as I sat down on an imitation-leather banquette at the other end of the room. From there I was able to watch him without his noticing my gaze. He spoke to them in a low voice, leaning toward them. Was he worried I would hear what he was saying? Then, to pass the time, I imagined all of the phrases I might have spoken in a feignedly urbane tone that would have made drops of sweat bead up on his forehead. "Are you still a doctor?" And then, after a long pause, "Say, are you still practicing at Quai Louis-Blériot? At least tell me you've kept your office on rue de Moscou. And that trip to Fresnes way back when, I hope there weren't too many serious consequences." I very nearly burst out laughing, all by myself in my corner. We never grow up. As the years go by, many people and many things end up seeming so humorous and so pathetic that all you can do is try to look at them through the eyes of a child.

That first visit, I spent a long time waiting at the Condé. She didn't come. I would have to be patient. It would wait for another day. I watched the customers. Most of them weren't more than twenty-five years old. A nineteenth-century novelist might have described them as "the student bohemians." But few of them, in my opinion, were enrolled at the Sorbonne or the École des Mines. I must admit that watching them up close, I didn't have high hopes for their futures.

Two men came in, one shortly after the other. Adamov and the dark-haired fellow with the flowing walk who had written a few books under the name Maurice Raphaël. I knew Adamov at first sight. In bygone days, he was almost always at the Old Navy Café, and his stare was one you didn't forget. I believe I had done him a favor to help sort out his living situation, back when I still had a few contacts at the Renseignements Généraux. As for Maurice Raphaël, he too was a regular in the bars of the area. I've heard that he had been in some trouble after the war under a different name. Back in those days, I was working for Blémant. They both came up and leaned their elbows on the bar. Maurice Raphaël remained standing, rather stiffly, and Adamov hauled himself up onto a barstool, wincing in pain. He hadn't yet remarked my presence. Would my face still bring anything back for him? Three young people, including a blond girl with bangs wearing a worn raincoat, joined them at the bar. Maurice Raphaël held out a pack of cigarettes and looked at them with an amused smile. Adamov showed himself to be less at ease with them. His intense stare made you think he was somewhat frightened by them.

I had two photo-booth pictures of this Jacqueline Delanque in my pocket. Back when I worked for Blémant, he had always been surprised at how easily I could identify someone. All it took was for my eyes to pass over a face once for it to remain engraved in my memory. Blémant had often kidded me about my ability to immediately recognize someone from afar, whether it was in three-quarter profile or even from behind. So I wasn't the least bit worried. As soon as she came into the Condé, I would know it was her.

Dr. Vala turned towards the bar and our eyes met. He gave a friendly wave. I suddenly had the urge to walk over to his table and tell him that I had a private question to ask him. I would have taken him aside and showed him the photos. "You know her?" Really, it would have been helpful to find out a bit more about this girl from one of the customers at the Condé.

As soon as I learned the address of her hotel, I had made my way there. I had chosen the middle of the afternoon, as it would be more likely that she was out. At least so I hoped. Then I would be able to ask the front desk a few questions about her. It was a sunny autumn day and I decided to make the trek on foot. I set out from the quays and slowly made my way inland. By rue du Cherche-Midi, the sun was in my eyes. I went into Au Chien Qui Fume and ordered a cognac. I was anxious. I surveyed avenue du Maine from the window. All I needed to do was to walk down the left sidewalk and I'd reach my destination. No reason to feel anxious. As I continued along the avenue, I regained my calm. I was nearly certain she wouldn't be there, and in any case, I wouldn't go into the hotel to ask questions this time, I would wander around outside as if I were on a stakeout. I had plenty of time. I had been paid for it.

When I reached rue Cels, I decided to be clear in my mind about things. A calm and gray street, it reminded me not only of a village or a suburb but of those mysterious regions they call "the borderlands." I went straight to the front desk. No one. I waited about ten minutes, hoping that she wouldn't appear. A door opened and a woman with short dark hair, dressed all in black, came to the reception desk. I said in a pleasant voice: "This is regarding Jacqueline Delanque."

I figured she had registered here under her maiden name.

She smiled at me and took an envelope from one of the pigeonholes behind her.

"Are you Monsieur Roland?"

Now who was this? Just in case, I gave a vague nod of the head. She handed me the envelope, on which was written in blue ink: "For Roland." The envelope wasn't sealed. On a large sheet of paper, I read:

Roland, come and meet me after five o'clock at the Condé. If you can't, call me at AUTEUIL 15-28 and leave me a message.

It was signed "Louki." A pet name for Jacqueline?

I folded the sheet up and slid it into the envelope, handing it back to the brunette.

"Excuse me. There's been a mix-up. This isn't for me."

She didn't react at all but mechanically replaced the letter in the pigeonhole.

"Has Jacqueline Delanque lived here a long time?"

She hesitated a moment and then replied affably, "For about a month."

"Alone?"

"Yes."

She seemed indifferent to me and ready to answer all of my questions. She gave me a weary look.

"Thank you very much," I said to her.

"You're welcome."

I didn't want to linger, as this Roland could arrive at any time. I went back out onto avenue du Maine and followed it in the direction from which I'd come. At Au Chien Qui Fume, I ordered another cognac. I looked up the Condé's address in the directory. It was in the Quartier de l'Odéon. Four o'clock in the afternoon, I had a bit of time to kill, so I placed a call to AUTEUIL 15-28. A terse voice that reminded me of a speaking clock: "La Fontaine Garage, how can I help you?" I asked for Jacqueline Delanque. "She's stepped out a moment. Can I take a message?" I was tempted to hang up, but I forced myself to reply. "No, no message. Thank you."

Above all, it's necessary to determine people's itineraries with as much precision as possible in order to understand them better. I repeated to myself, in a low voice: "Hotel rue Cels. La Fontaine Garage. Café Condé. Louki." And then, that part of Neuilly between the Bois de Boulogne and the Seine, where that fellow had asked me to meet him to talk about his wife, the aforementioned Jacqueline Choureau, née Delanque.

I can't remember who recommended that he talk to me. It doesn't really matter. He probably found my address in the directory. I had taken the Métro well before the appointed time. It was a direct line. I got off at Sablons and walked around for nearly half an hour. I had a habit of getting to know the lay of the land before jumping straight into the thick of things. In the past, Blémant criticized me for it and thought that I was wasting my time. Dive in, he told me, rather than running in circles around the edge of the pool. Personally, I felt the opposite way. No sudden movements, but instead a passivity and slowness that allow you to be softly penetrated by the spirit of the place.

The scents of autumn and the country were in the air. I followed the avenue that ran along the Jardin d'Acclimatation, only I stuck to the other side next to the Bois de Boulogne and the bridle path. I would have loved it if it were just a casual stroll.

This Jean-Pierre Choureau had called me to set up a meeting, his voice devoid of expression. All he let me know was that it was about his wife. As I approached his home, I saw him walking along the bridle path, as I was, passing the amusement rides of the Jardin d'Acclimatation. How old was he? The timbre of his voice had seemed youthful to me, but voices can often be misleading.

What drama or marital hell would he drag me into? I felt assailed by discouragement, and I wasn't completely sure I wanted to go to this meeting. I headed across the Bois towards the Mare Saint-James and the small lake the ice skaters frequented during the winter. I was the only one walking there and I got the impression that I was far from Paris, maybe somewhere in Sologne. Once again, I managed to overcome the discouragement. A vague professional curiosity made me interrupt my stroll through the woods and return towards the outskirts of Neuilly. Sologne. Neuilly. I imagined long rainy afternoons in Neuilly for the Choureaus. And over there, in Sologne, you could hear the horns of the hunt at dusk. Did his wife ride sidesaddle? I burst out laughing as I remembered Blémant's remark: "Caisley, you go way too far, way too fast. You ought to have been a novelist."

He lived at the far end, by the Porte de Madrid, in a modern building with a large windowed entrance. He had told me to go to the end of the hall and then to turn left. I would see his name on the door. "It's an apartment on the ground floor." I had been surprised by the sadness with which he had said "ground floor." Then there was a long silence, as if he regretted the admission.

"And the exact address?" I had asked him.

"Eleven, avenue de Bretteville. Have you got that? Eleven. At four o'clock, would that work for you?"

His voice had grown steadier, taking on an almost conversational tone.

The small golden plaque on the door read "Jean-Pierre Choureau," over which I noticed a peephole. I rang. I waited. There, in that deserted and silent hallway, I told myself that I had come too late. He had committed suicide. I felt ashamed by such a thought and, once again, I had a strong desire to drop the whole thing, to leave that hall, to return to my walk in the fresh air, in Sologne. I rang again, this time in three short bursts. The door opened straight away, as if he had been stationed behind it, observing me through the peephole.

A man of some forty years, with short-cropped brown hair, well above average height. He wore a navy blue suit and a sky blue shirt, the collar open. He led me wordlessly towards what one might have referred to as the living room. He motioned to a sofa behind a coffee table, and we sat down side by side. He struggled to speak. To put him at ease, I said to him, in the softest voice possible, "So this is about your wife?"

He tried to take on a detached tone, shooting me a lifeless smile. Yes, his wife had disappeared two months ago after an unspectacular argument. Could I be the first person that he had spoken to since her disappearance? The iron shutter of one of the bay windows was lowered, and I wondered if this man had cloistered himself in his apartment for the past two months. But other than the shutter, there was no trace of disorder or sloppiness in the living room. As for him, after wavering for a moment, he regained a certain self-composure.

"I would like this situation to be cleared up rather quickly," he finally told me.

I took a closer look at him. Very light-colored eyes below black brows, high cheekbones, unremarkable features. In his appearance and his way of moving, there was an athletic vigor that was accentuated by his short hair. You could have easily imagined him on a sailboat, shirtless, a solitary navigator. And in spite of such apparent vitality and charm, his wife had left him.

I wanted to know whether during all that time he had made any attempts to find her. No. She had telephoned him three or four times, letting him know that she would not be coming back. She had strongly advised against his trying to get in touch with her and gave him no explanation. Her voice had changed. This was no longer even the same person. A very calm voice, very confident, a change that he had found quite disconcerting. He and his wife were almost fifteen years apart in age. She, twenty-two. He, thirty-six. As he gave me those details, I felt about him a certain distance, even a coldness, clearly the fruit of what one would call a proper education. And now I needed to ask him questions that were increasingly specific and I no longer knew if it was worth the trouble. What exactly was it that he wanted? For his wife to return? Or was he simply seeking to understand why she had left him? Perhaps this would be enough for him. With the exception of the sofa and coffee table, there was no furniture in the living room. The bay windows gave on to the avenue where cars passed by only occasionally, so infrequently that the ground-floor level of the apartment wasn't a concern. Night was falling. He lit the red-shaded tripod lamp that stood next to the sofa on my right. The light made me blink my eyes, a white light that made the silence even more profound. I think he was waiting for my questions. He had crossed his legs. To buy some time, I took my spiral-bound notebook and my ballpoint pen from the inside pocket of my coat and made a few notes. "Him, 36 yrs old. Her, 22. Neuilly. First-floor apartment. No furniture. Bay windows looking onto avenue de Bretteville. No traffic. A few magazines on the coffee table." He waited without saying a thing as if I were a doctor writing a prescription.

"Your wife's maiden name?"

"Delanque. Jacqueline Delanque."

I asked him the date and place of birth of this Jacqueline Delanque. The date, also, of their marriage. Did she have a driver's license? A steady job? No. Did she have any family left? In Paris? In the provinces? A checkbook? As he answered me in a sad voice, I jotted down all of those details that are often the sole things that bear witness to the passage of a human being on Earth. Provided that one day someone finds the spiral-bound notebook in which they were recorded in a tiny, difficult-to-read script such as my own.

Now it was necessary for me to move on to more delicate questions, the ones that grant access to a man's private life without first having to ask his permission. What gives us the right?

"You have friends?"

Yes, a few people that he saw regularly enough. He knew them from business school. A few had also been classmates at the Lycée Jean-Baptiste Say.

He had even tried to open a firm with three of them before going to work for the Zannetacci Real Estate Company as an active partner.

"Are you still working?"

"Yes. At 20, rue de la Paix."

What means of transportation did he use when he went to the office? Every detail, no matter how trivial it may seem, is telling. By automobile. He traveled for Zannetacci from time to time. Lyon. Bordeaux. The Côte d'Azur. Geneva. And Jacqueline Choureau, née Delanque, did she stay behind on her own in Neuilly? He had taken her along on these trips a few times, they had gone to the Côte d'Azur. And when she was on her own, what did she do with her free time? There truly wasn't anyone who might be able to give him information concerning the disappearance of Jacqueline, married name Choureau, born Delanque, to give him the slightest clue? "I don't know, a secret she might have told you one day when she was feeling blue?" "No. She would never have confided in anyone." Often, she reproached him for his friends' total lack of imagination. It was important to keep in mind, as well, that she was nearly fifteen years younger than they were.

I had now arrived at a question that already bothered me a great deal, but one that it was necessary to ask: "Do you think she had a lover?"

The tone of my voice struck me as a bit brutal and a bit stupid. But that's how it was. He frowned.

"No."

He hesitated, he looked me right in the eye as if he was waiting for encouragement from me or as if he was searching for the right words. One evening, one of his old business-school friends had come to their place for dinner and had brought along someone called Guy de Vere, a man older than the rest of them. This Guy de Vere was very well versed in the occult sciences and had offered to bring them a few works on the subject. His wife had attended several gatherings and even some sort of conference given regularly by this Guy de Vere. He hadn't been able to accompany her due to a backlog of work at Zannetacci. His wife developed an interest in these gatherings and spoke of them often, without him really understanding what they were all about. She had borrowed one of the books that Guy de Vere had suggested to her, the one that had seemed the easiest to read. It was called *Lost Horizon*. Had he been in contact with Guy de Vere after his wife's disappearance? Yes, he had telephoned him several times, but de Vere didn't know anything. "Are you positive about that?" He shrugged his shoulders and fixed me with a weary look. This Guy de Vere had been very evasive and it had been clear that he would get no information from him. The exact name and address of this man? He didn't know his address, it wasn't in the directory.

I tried to think of other questions to ask him. A moment of silence passed between us, but it didn't appear to bother him. Seated side by side on that sofa, it was as if we were in a dentist's or a doctor's waiting room. White, bare walls. A woman's portrait hung over the sofa. I nearly picked up one of the magazines from the coffee table. A sense of emptiness came over me. I must admit that at that moment I felt the absence of Jacqueline Choureau née Delanque to the point that it felt definitive to me. But there was no reason to be a pessimist right from the start. And further, wouldn't this living room have had the same feeling of emptiness even if the woman had been present? Did they dine there? If so, it must have been on a card table that was folded up and put away afterwards. I wanted to know if she had left on the spur of the moment, without bothering to take all of her belongings. No. She had taken her clothing and the few books Guy de Vere had lent her, all of it in a dark red leather suitcase. There wasn't the slightest trace of her. Even the pictures with her in them—a few vacation photos—had disappeared. Evenings, alone in the apartment, he wondered if he had ever been married to Jacqueline Delanque. The sole remaining proof was the family record book given to them after they had married. Family record book. He repeated these words as if he didn't understand their meaning.

It was pointless for me to visit the other rooms of the apartment. Empty rooms. Empty closets. And silence, barely disturbed by the passing of a car on avenue de Bretteville. The evenings must have been long.

"Did she take a key with her?"

He shook his head no. Not even the hope of one night hearing the sound of the key in the lock that would announce her return. And he didn't think it likely that she would ever call again.

"How did you two meet?"

She had been hired at Zannetacci to fill in for an employee. Temporary secretarial work. He had dictated a few client letters to her and that's how they had gotten to know each other. They had seen each other outside of the office. She told him that she was a student at the École des Langues Orientales, where she took classes twice a week, but he never found out exactly which language she had been studying. Asian languages, she said. And, after two months, they were married one Saturday morning at the city hall in Neuilly, with two colleagues from Zannetacci as witnesses. No one else attended what was for him a simple formality. They had gone to lunch with the witnesses right near his place, just outside the Bois de Boulogne, at a restaurant often frequented by customers from the neighboring amusement park.

He shot me an embarrassed look. Apparently he had wanted to give me a more detailed account of their marriage. I smiled at him. I didn't need an explanation. Making an effort he took the plunge: "It's all about trying to create ties, you see."

Well, sure, I understood. In this life that sometimes seems to be a vast, ill-defined landscape without signposts, amid all of the vanishing lines and the lost horizons, we hope to find reference points, to draw up some sort of land registry so as to shake the impression that we are navigating by chance. So we forge ties, we try to find stability in chance encounters. I kept quiet, my gaze fixed on the stack of magazines. In the middle of the coffee table sat a large yellow ashtray that bore the inscription "Cinzano." And a paperback book entitled *Fare Thee Well, Focolara.* Zannetacci. Jean-Pierre Choureau. Cinzano. Jacqueline Delanque. Neuilly City Hall. Focolara. As if we were supposed to find some sense in all of this.

"And of course she was terribly charming. I fell head over heels for her."

As soon as he had made this admission in a low voice, he seemed to regret it. In the days leading up to her disappearance, had he noticed anything different about her? Well sure, she complained to him more and more about their daily lives. This wasn't what it was supposed to be like, she said, real life. And when he asked her what it really consisted of, this "real life," she shrugged her shoulders without answering, as if she knew that he wouldn't understand her explanation. And then she found her smile once again, and her kindness, and she was almost apologetic for her bad mood. With a look of resignation, she told him that in the end it wasn't so bad. One day, maybe, he would understand what "real life" was.

"You really don't have a single photograph of her?"

One afternoon, they were walking along the Seine. He

had planned on taking the Métro to Châtelet to get to the office. On the boulevard du Palais, they passed a little photo-booth kiosk. She needed photos for a new passport. He waited for her on the sidewalk. When she came out, she had handed him the photos, telling him that she was afraid she would lose them. Once back at the office, he had put the photos in an envelope and had forgotten to bring them back to Neuilly. After his wife's disappearance, he had noticed that the envelope was still there, on his desk, among the administrative documents.

"Would you excuse me a moment?"

He left me alone on the sofa. It was dark out. I looked at my watch and I was surprised that the hands only showed a quarter to six. It felt like I had been there much longer.

Two pictures in a gray envelope, on the left of which was printed: "Zannetacci Real Estate, 20, rue de la Paix, Paris 1st." One shot head on, one in profile, the kind they still insisted on for foreigners at the police headquarters. Her family name, Delanque, and her first name, Jacqueline, were very French all the same. Two pictures that I held between thumb and index finger as I contemplated them in silence. Brown hair, pale-colored eyes, and one of those profiles so unsullied that it gave off charm even in an anthropometric photo. And those two pictures had all the dinginess and all the coldness common to anthropometric photos.

"Lend them to me for a while?" I asked him.

"Of course."

I stuffed the envelope into a jacket pocket.

There comes a time when you have to stop listening to other people. What did he, Jean-Pierre Choureau, really know about Jacqueline Delanque? Not much. They had lived together for barely a year in this street-level apartment in Neuilly. They had sat side by side on this sofa, they had eaten across from each other, and once in a while they had dined with old friends from business school and from the Lycée Jean-Baptiste Say. Is that enough to guess the entirety of what goes on in someone's head? Did she still see any family relations? I made one final effort to ask him this question.

"No, she didn't have any family left."

I got up. He gave me an anxious look. He remained seated on the sofa.

"It's time I get going," I told him. "It's late."

I smiled at him, but he seemed surprised that I wanted to take my leave of him.

"I'll call you as soon as possible," I told him. "I hope to be able to give you some news before too long."

He got up in turn, with the same trancelike movements he had used to guide me to the living room earlier. One final question came to mind.

"Did she have any money when she left?"

"No."

"And when she called you, once she had left, did she give you any indication as to how she was getting by?"

"No."

He walked towards the front door with his stiff gait. Would he still be able to answer my questions? I opened the door. He stood behind me, frozen. I don't know what it was that came over me, what disequilibrium or rush of bitterness, but I said to him in an aggressive tone: "I'd imagine you had hoped you would grow old together?"

Was this to wake him from his torpor and depression? His eyes widened and he stared at me with fear. I stood in the doorframe. I stepped closer to him and put my hand on his shoulder.

"Don't hesitate to call me. Any time of day."

His face relaxed. He managed a smile. Before closing the door, he waved goodbye. I remained a long moment on the landing, and the automatic lighting went out. I imagined him sitting alone on the sofa, in the position he had occupied earlier. Absentmindedly picking up a magazine from the stack on the coffee table.

It was dark outside. I couldn't pull my thoughts away from this man in his ground-floor apartment, sitting under the stark light of the lamp. Would he have something to eat before he went to bed? I wondered if he had a kitchen in there. I should have invited him for dinner. Perhaps, without me asking him questions, he might have said something, an admission that would have put me on the trail of Jacqueline Delanque more quickly. Blémant often told me that there comes a time for each individual, even the most stubborn, when he "spills the beans." That was his motto. It was for us to await this moment with the utmost patience, while trying, of course, to provoke it, but in an almost imperceptible manner, as Blémant said, "with delicate little pinpricks." The fellow must feel as if he is before a confessor. It's tricky. That's the job. I had reached the Porte-Maillot and I felt like walking for a while yet in the mildness of the evening. Unfortunately, my new shoes were really hurting my insteps. And so, back on the avenue, I went into the first café and selected one of the tables nearest the bay windows. I untied my shoes and removed the left one, the one that was causing me the most pain. When the waiter came, I didn't even try to resist a brief moment of forgetfulness and relaxation, and I asked for an Izarra Verte.

I took the envelope from my pocket and I pored over the pictures for a long while. Where was she now? In a café, like me, sitting alone at a table? Doubtless the phrase he had spoken earlier had given me this idea: "It's all about trying to create ties." Encounters in the street, in a Métro station at rush hour. We ought to shackle ourselves to each other at that moment. What connection can resist the tide as it carries you away and diverts your course? An anonymous office where you dictate a letter to a temp typist, a ground-floor apartment in Neuilly whose white, empty walls evoke what some would call a "showroom apartment," where there would be no trace left of your stay. Two photo-booth snapshots, one facing the camera, one in profile. And that's what we're supposed to forge links with? There was someone who would be able to help me with my search: Bernolle. I hadn't seen him since my Blémant days, except for one afternoon about three years ago. I was on my way to the Métro and I was crossing the square in front of Notre-Dame. A tramp came out of the Hôtel-Dieu and our paths crossed. He was wearing a raincoat with torn sleeves, pants that stopped above the ankles, and his bare feet were wedged into a pair of old sandals. He was unshaven and his dark hair was too long. And yet I recognized him. Bernolle. I followed him with the intention of speaking to him. But he was walking too quickly. He went in the front door of the police headquarters. I hesitated a moment. It was too late to catch him, so I decided to wait right there on the sidewalk. After all, we had grown up together.

He came back out of the same door in a navy blue coat, flannel pants, and black lace-up shoes. It was no longer the same man. He seemed nervous when I approached him. He was freshly shaven. We walked the length of the quay without saying a word. Once we had taken a seat at a table a bit farther down, at the Soleil d'Or, he confided in me. He was still employed digging up information, oh, nothing big, some work as an informant and a mole where he played the part of a tramp to better see and hear what went on around him: staking out building fronts, the various flea markets, Pigalle, around the train stations, and even in the Latin Quarter. He had a sad smile. He lived in a studio in the sixteenth arrondissement. He gave me his telephone number. Not for a moment did we speak of the past. He had placed his travel bag on the bench next to him. He would have been rather surprised if I had told him what it contained: an old raincoat, pants that were too short, a pair of sandals.

The very evening I returned from the meeting in Neuilly, I telephoned him. Ever since we had reconnected, I occasionally turned to him for information I required. I asked him to find me some details concerning one Jacqueline Delanque, married name Choureau. I didn't have much else to tell him about this person, other than her date of birth and that of her marriage to a certain Choureau, Jean-Pierre, of 11, avenue de Bretteville in Neuilly, an active partner with Zannetacci. He took notes. "That's all?" He seemed disappointed. "And nothing on either of them in the criminal records, I suppose," he said in a disdainful voice. "No rap sheets?" Criminal records. Rap sheets. I tried to picture the Choureaus' bedroom in Neuilly, the bedroom I ought to have taken a look at out of professional conscientiousness.

A bedroom empty forevermore, a bare mattress stripped of its sheets.

Over the course of the following weeks, Choureau telephoned me several times. He always spoke in an expressionless voice and it was always seven o'clock in the evening. Perhaps at that particular hour, alone in his ground-floor apartment, he felt the need to talk to someone. I told him to be patient. I got the feeling that he had given up and that he would slowly begin to accept his wife's disappearance. I received a letter from Bernolle:

My dear Caisley,

No jacket on file in the criminal records. Neither under Choureau nor Delanque.

But chance is a strange mistress. A tedious statistical assignment that I've been working on within the police station logs of the 9th and 18th arrondissements led me to find you a bit of information.

On two separate occasions, I came across "Delanque, Jacqueline, 15 years old." The first time, in the logs of the Quartier Saint-Georges police station, from seven years ago, and a second time, several months later, in that of Grandes-Carrières. Grounds: Juvenile Vagrancy.

I asked at Leoni if there might be something concerning hotels. Two years ago, Delanque, Jacqueline, lived at the Hôtel San Remo, 8, rue d'Armaillé (17th) and the Hôtel Métropole, 13, rue de l'Étoile (17th). In the logs from Saint-Georges and from Grandes-

Carrières, it indicates that she lived with her mother at 10, avenue Rachel (18th arrondissement).

She currently lives at the Hôtel Savoie, 8, rue Cels, in the 14th arrondissement. Her mother passed away four years ago. On her birth certificate from the city hall in Fontaines-en-Sologne (Loir-et-Cher), of which I am sending you a copy, it indicates that she was born to an unknown father. Her mother was employed as an usher at the Moulin Rouge and had a friend, a Guy Lavigne, who worked at the La Fontaine Garage (16th) and who helped her out financially. Jacqueline Delanque doesn't seem to have steady employment.

There, my dear Caisley, you have everything that I have gathered for you. I hope to see you soon, but on the condition that it isn't in my work attire. Blémant would have laughed heartily at that tramp disguise. You, a little less, I suppose. And me, not a bit.

Take care,

Bernolle

All that remained was for me to telephone Jean-Pierre Choureau and tell him that the mystery was cleared up. I'm trying to remember at which exact moment I decided not to do anything about it. I had dialed the first digits of his number when I hung up abruptly. I was overwhelmed at the thought of going back to that ground-floor apartment in Neuilly during the late afternoon as I had before, of waiting with him under the red-shaded lamp for night to fall. I unfolded the old Taride map of Paris that I always keep on my desk, within arm's reach. Through my years of consulting it, I have often torn it at the edges, and each time, I stuck Scotch tape over the tear, as if I were dressing a wound. The Condé. Neuilly. Quartier de l'Étoile. Avenue Rachel. For the first time in my professional life, I felt the need to go against the tide while conducting my investigation. Yes, I was traveling the road that Jacqueline Delanque had followed, but in the opposite direction. Jean-Pierre Choureau no longer mattered. He had only been a bit part and I saw him receding into the distance forever, a black briefcase in his hand, towards the Zannetacci offices. In the end, the only interesting person was Jacqueline Delanque. There had been many Jacquelines in my life. She would be the last. I took the Métro, the north-south line, as they call it, the one that connected avenue Rachel to the Condé. As the stations passed by, I traveled back in time. I got off at Pigalle. Once there, I walked along the boulevard's wide median with a spring in my step. A sunny autumn afternoon where it would have been nice to work on new projects and where life could have started over from scratch. After all, it was in this area that her life had begun, this Jacqueline Delanque. It seemed as if she and I had an appointment. Coming up on place Blanche, my heart was racing a bit and I felt nervous and even intimidated. I hadn't felt this way in a long time. I continued on down the median, my pace growing quicker. I could have walked this familiar district with my eyes closed: the Moulin Rouge, Le Sanglier Bleu. Who knows? Maybe I had crossed paths with this Jacqueline Delanque a long time ago, on the right-hand sidewalk as she went to meet her mother at the Moulin Rouge, or on the opposite side as school let out from the Lycée Jules-Ferry. There, I had arrived. I had forgotten about the cinema on the corner of the avenue. It was called the Mexico, and it wasn't by chance that it had such a name. It gave you the desire to travel, to run away, to disappear. I had also forgotten the silence and calm of avenue Rachel, which leads to the cemetery, although you never think of the cemetery, you tell yourself that at its end it must let out onto the countryside, or even, with a bit of luck, onto a seaside promenade.

I stopped in front of number 10 and, after a moment of hesitation, I went into the building. I went to knock on the concierge's glass door, but I stopped myself. What good would that do? On a little sign glued to one of the door's panes were listed the names of the tenants and the floor number of each one. I took my notebook and my ballpoint pen from the inside pocket of my jacket and made note of the names:

Deyrlord (Christiane)
Dix (Gisèle)
Dupuy (Marthe)
Esnault (Yvette)
Gravier (Alice)
Manoury (Albine)
Mariska
Van Bosterhaudt (Huguette)
Zazani (Odette)

The name Delanque (Geneviève) was crossed out and replaced by Van Bosterhaudt (Huguette). The mother and daughter had lived on the fifth floor. Yet as I closed my notebook I knew that none of these details would do me any good.

Outside, by the building's entrance, a man stood on the doorstep of a fabric shop whose sign read La Licorne. As I was looking up towards the fifth floor, I heard him say to me in a reedy voice, "Can I help you find something, sir?"

I ought to have asked him about Geneviève and Jacqueline Delanque, but I knew how he would have responded, nothing but very superficial little "surface" details, as Blémant used to say, without ever getting to the heart of the matter. All it took was to hear his reedy voice, to notice his weaselly face and the severity of his stare: No, there was nothing to hope for from him, except for the "information" that you could get from any old informant. Or else he would tell me that he didn't know Geneviève or Jacqueline Delanque. A cold rage swept over me, directed at this weasel-faced fellow. Perhaps he suddenly took the place of all the so-called witnesses I had interrogated during my investigations, people who had never understood a thing of what they had seen, be it out of stupidity, spite, or sheer indifference. I walked with a heavy step and planted myself in front of him. I was some eight inches taller than him and weighed twice what he did.

"Is it against the law to look at a building?"

He stared at me with severe and timorous eyes. I would have liked to scare him even more.

And then, to calm myself, I sat down on a bench on the median, up by the entrance to the avenue, across from the Cinéma Mexico. I took off my left shoe.

Sunshine. I was lost in my thoughts. Jacqueline Delanque could count on my discretion, Choureau would never learn anything of the Hôtel Savoie, the Condé, La Fontaine Garage, or this person named Roland, doubtless the brown-haired guy in the suede jacket mentioned in the notebook. "Louki. Monday, February 12th, 11 p.m. Louki, April 28th, 2 p.m. Louki with the brown-haired guy in the suede jacket." Throughout the pages of the notebook, I had underlined her name each time in blue pencil and recopied all the notes that concerned her on loose sheets. With the dates. And the times. But she had no reason to worry. I wouldn't go back to the Condé. Really, I had been fortunate, the two or three times I had waited for her at one of the tables in the café, that she hadn't come on those days. I would have been embarrassed to spy on her without her knowing, yes, I would have been ashamed of my role. By what right do we intrude, forcing our way in like common crooks, and by what presumptuousness do we delve into their heads and their hearts—and ask them to account for themselves? By what authority? I had taken off my shoe and was massaging my instep. The pain died down. Night fell. Before, I suppose this would have been about the time Geneviève Delanque left for work at the Moulin Rouge. Her daughter stayed home alone, on the fifth floor. Towards thirteen, fourteen years old, one evening, once her mother had gone, she had left the building, careful not to be noticed by the concierge. Outside, she hadn't gone past the street corner. She had been happy, the first several times, with the ten o'clock show at the Cinéma Mexico. Then the return trip to the building, climbing the stairs without setting off the automatic lights, the door shut as softly as possible. One night, when the cinema let out, she had walked a little farther, as far as place Blanche. And each night, a little bit farther. Juvenile Vagrancy, it had been written in the police logs of the Quartier Saint-Georges and in those of Grandes-Carrières, and those two words evoked for me a meadow beneath the moon, beyond the Caulaincourt bridge all the way back there, behind the cemetery, a meadow where at last you could breathe in the fresh air.

Her mother had come to pick her up at the police station. Unfortunately, things had already been set in motion and no one could hold her back any longer. Nocturnal wandering towards the west, if I was correctly reading the few clues that Bernolle had gathered. At first, the Quartier de l'Étoile, and then still farther west, Neuilly and the Bois de Boulogne. But why, then, had she married Choureau? And once again flight, but this time towards the Rive Gauche, as if crossing the river would protect her from some imminent danger. And yet hadn't this marriage also been a kind of protection? If she'd had the patience to stay in Neuilly, it would have eventually been forgotten that beneath a Madame Jean-Pierre Choureau hid a Jacqueline Delanque whose name appeared in the police logs on two occasions.

Evidently I was once again a prisoner of my old professional conditioning, habits that made my colleagues believe that, even as I slept, I carried out my investigations. Blémant compared me to the postwar gangster they called "the Man Who Smokes in His Sleep." He always kept an ashtray on the edge of his night table upon which he rested a lit cigarette. He slept in fits and starts, and each time he was briefly awake, he stretched an arm over to the ashtray and inhaled a puff of cigarette. Then, as if in a trance, he would light another one. And yet in the morning, he had no recollection of any of it and was convinced he had slept deeply. On that bench, I too, now that night had fallen, had the impression of being in a dream in which I continued to follow Jacqueline Delanque's trail.

Or to be more precise, I felt her presence on this boulevard, its lights shining like signals without my being able to decipher them very well. They spoke to me from the depths of the years, but I didn't know which ones. And these lights, they seemed even more vivid to me from the dimness of the median. Vivid and distant at the same time.

I had slipped my sock back on, and once again stuffed my foot into my left shoe, getting up from the bench where I would gladly have spent the whole night. And I walked along the wide median as she had, at fifteen, before she had been picked up. Where and at which moment had she attracted attention?

Jean-Pierre Choureau would eventually grow weary. I would answer his telephone calls a few more times, feeding him vague information—all false, of course. Paris is big and it's quite easy to lose someone in it. Once I got the feeling that I had set him on the wrong track, I would stop taking his calls. Jacqueline could count on me. I would give her the time to put herself out of reach for good.

At this moment, she too was walking somewhere in this city. Or maybe she was sitting at a table, at the Condé. But she had nothing to fear. I would no longer be at our rendez-vous.

WHEN I was fifteen years old, you would have thought I was nineteen, even twenty. My name wasn't Louki then, it was Jacqueline. I was even younger than fifteen the first time I took advantage of my mother's absence to go out. She went to work around nine o'clock in the evening and she didn't come back before two in the morning. That first time, I had prepared a lie in case the concierge caught me in the stairwell. I was going to tell him that I needed to purchase some medicine from the pharmacy at place Blanche.

I hadn't been back to the neighborhood until the night Roland took me, by taxi, to the home of one of Guy de Vere's friends. We were going there to meet everyone who regularly attended the lectures. We had only recently met at that point, Roland and I, and I wasn't comfortable saying something when he had the taxi stop at place Blanche. He wanted us to walk a ways. Perhaps he didn't notice how tightly I held on to his arm. I was overcome by dizziness. I had the feeling that if I crossed the square, I would faint dead away. I was afraid. The way he always talked about the Eternal Return, I'm sure he would have understood. Yes, everything was beginning over again for me. It was as if meeting up with these people was only a pretext, as if Roland had been entrusted with bringing me gently back into the fold.

I had been relieved when we didn't go past the Moulin Rouge. And yet my mother had already been dead four years at that point and I had nothing left to worry about. Each time that I would slip out of the apartment at night, in her absence, I walked on the other side of the boulevard, the side that lay in the ninth arrondissement. There wasn't a single streetlight on that sidewalk. The lightless building that was the Lycée Jules-Ferry, then the façades of apartment buildings, their windows dim, and a restaurant, although it always seemed as if its dining room was kept in perpetual darkness. And, each time, I was unable to stop myself from looking at the Moulin Rouge that lay on the other side of the median. When I had drawn even with the Café des Palmiers and came out onto place Blanche, I still wasn't terribly reassured. All of those bright lights, once again. One night as I passed the pharmacy, I had seen my mother through the window with some other customers. I had realized that she had finished work earlier than usual and would soon be heading back to the apartment. If I ran, I could make it back before her. I had stationed myself at the corner of rue de Bruxelles to find out which route she would take. But she had crossed the square and had returned to the Moulin Rouge.

I was often frightened, and to reassure myself I would have gladly gone to see my mother, but I would have been disturbing her at work. Thinking back, I'm certain she wouldn't have scolded me, because the night she came to pick me up at the Grandes-Carrières police station, she hadn't offered the least reproach, no threats, no discipline whatsoever. We walked in silence. Halfway across the Caulaincourt bridge, I heard her say, in a detached voice, "My poor little darling," but I wasn't sure if she was speaking to me or talking to herself. She waited for me to undress and climb into bed before she came into my room. She sat down at the foot of the bed and remained silent. As did I. Eventually she started smiling. "We're not very talkative, are we?" she said, and she looked me straight in the eye. It was the first time her gaze had lingered on me so long, and the first time I noticed how light her eyes were, gray, or a washed-out blue. Blue-gray. She leaned down and kissed me on the cheek, or rather I very briefly felt her lips. And still that stare fixed on me, those clear and distant eyes. She turned out the light, and before she closed the door, she told me, "Let's try not to have any more of that." I think that's the only time we ever really connected, and it was so fleeting, so awkward, and yet so strong that I regret it didn't propel me towards her during the months that followed that night in a way that might have brought about that contact again. But neither of us was a very demonstrative person. Perhaps as far as I was concerned, she had adopted that seemingly indifferent attitude because she had no illusions whatsoever when it came to me. She likely figured there wasn't much use in getting her hopes up considering how alike we were.

But none of that ever crossed my mind at the time. I was living in the present without much in the way of soul-searching. All of that changed the night Roland made me return to the old neighborhood I had been avoiding. I hadn't set foot in it since my mother's death. The taxi had turned onto rue de la Chaussée-d'Antin and, way down at the end, I could see the dark bulk of the Église de la Sainte-Trinité, like a gigantic eagle standing guard. I felt ill. We were getting close to the boundary. I told myself there was still a chance. Maybe we were going to turn right. But no.

We drove straight on ahead, we passed the Square de la Trinité, we climbed the hill. At the red light before we arrived at place de Clichy, I very nearly threw open my car door to escape. But I couldn't do that to him.

It was a while later, as we walked along rue des Abbesses towards the building that was our destination, that I regained my composure. Fortunately, Roland hadn't noticed a thing. Since then, I've been disappointed that the two of us didn't spend more time walking in that neighborhood. I would have liked to show him around, to take him to see the place I lived in not quite six years ago, although it seems so long ago now, like it was in another life. After my mother died, only one link remained to tie me to that period, Guy Lavigne, a friend of my mother's. My understanding was that he was the one who had paid our rent. I still see him from time to time. He works in a garage in Auteuil. But we rarely speak about the past. He's about as talkative as my mother. When they picked me up and took me to the police station, they asked me a number of questions I was required to answer, but at first I did it with such reluctance that they said to me, "Well now, you aren't very talkative, are you?," just like they would have to my mother or Guy Lavigne had either of them ever been in their clutches. I wasn't used to people asking me questions. I was actually astonished that they had any interest in me in the first place. The second time, at the Grandes-Carrières police station, I had lucked into a nicer cop than the first one and I felt more comfortable with the way he asked me questions. For once, it was possible to confide in someone, to talk about myself, and someone sitting across from me was interested in my story. I was so unaccustomed to such a situation that I couldn't find the words to answer. Other than very specific questions. For example, "Where did you go to school?" The Daughters of Charity of Saint Vincent de Paul on rue Caulaincourt, and the École Communale on rue Antoinette. I was ashamed to tell him that I hadn't been accepted to Lycée Jules-Ferry, but I took a deep breath and made the admission. He leaned toward me, and in a soft voice, he said, "That's Lycée Jules-Ferry's bad luck now, isn't it?" And that surprised me so greatly that at first I felt like laughing. He was smiling at me and looking me right in the eye, a gaze as clear as my mother's, but more tender, more attentive. He also asked me about my family situation. I began to trust him and I managed to give him a few scant details: My mother came from a village in Sologne, where a Mr. Foucret, the manager of the Moulin Rouge, owned an estate. That was how she, at a very young age, had secured a job at that establishment. I didn't know who my father was. I had been born there, in Sologne, but we had never gone back. That's why my mother had always told me, "There's nothing left of our home there, not even the foundations." He listened to me and took the occasional note. For me, it was a completely new sensation; as I gave him all of those meager details, it was as if a weight was lifted from me. None of it concerned me any longer, I was talking about someone else, and I was relieved to see that he was taking notes. If everything was written in black and white, that meant that it was over, the same way names and dates are inscribed on headstones. And I spoke more and more quickly, the words came tumbling out: the Moulin Rouge, my mother, Guy Lavigne, the Lycée Jules-Ferry, Sologne. I had never been able to talk to anybody. What a relief I felt as all those words came rushing from my mouth. A segment of my life was drawing to a close, a life that had been imposed on me. From then on, I would be the one to decide my lot in life. Everything would begin anew as of today, and in order to set things in motion, I would have preferred it if he had crossed out everything he had just written. I was ready to give him other details and other names, to tell him about an imaginary family, the sort of family I might have had in my dreams.

Around two in the morning, my mother came to fetch me. He told her that it wasn't terribly serious. He was still fixing me with his attentive stare. Juvenile Vagrancy, that's what had been written in their logbook. A taxi was waiting for us outside. When he had questioned me about my schooling, I had forgotten to tell him that, for a couple of months, I had attended a school a little further down the very sidewalk that led past the police station. I would wait at the canteen until my mother came to pick me up towards the end of the afternoon. Sometimes she would turn up late, and I would wait, sitting on a bench on the median. It was while waiting there one day that I had first noticed the street had a different name on either side of the intersection. She had come to pick me up near the school that night as well, except this time at the police station. An odd little street, that one, with its two names, always seeming to want to play a role in my life.

My mother shot an anxious look at the taxi meter from time to time. She instructed the taxi driver to stop at the corner of rue Caulaincourt, and when she dug the coins out of her change purse, I understood that she had just enough to cover the fare. We did the rest of the trek on foot. I walked faster than her and was leaving her behind. Then I stopped so that she could catch up. From the bridge that overlooked the cemetery, we could see our apartment building down below us. We stopped there for a long while, and I got the impression she was catching her breath. "You walk too fast," she told me. I have since had a realization. Perhaps I was trying to incite her to go a bit beyond the sheltered life she led. If she hadn't died, I think I might have succeeded in helping her expand her horizons.

In the three or four years that followed, it was the same itineraries, the same streets, although I continued to go farther and farther. Those first few times, I hadn't even walked as far as place Blanche. I hardly even went all the way around the block. First that tiny cinema on the corner of the boulevard, a little ways down from our apartment building. The late show began at ten o'clock. Other than on Saturdays, it was empty. The films were set in far-off lands like Mexico and Arizona. I paid no attention to the plot, only the scenery interested me. Once I was back outside, I was left with a curious amalgam of Arizona and the boulevard de Clichy in my head. The coloring of the illuminated signs and the neon were the same as that in the film—orange, emerald green, midnight blue, sandy yellow—colors that were too violent and gave me the feeling I was still in the movie or in a dream. A dream or a nightmare, it depended on the evening. A nightmare at first, because I was afraid and I wasn't bold enough to go much farther. And that wasn't because of my mother. If she had caught me all alone on the boulevard at midnight, it's likely she wouldn't have chastised me. She would have told me to go back to the apartment, her voice calm, as if she wasn't the least bit surprised to see me outside at such a late hour. I think I usually walked on the opposite sidewalk, the one that lay hidden in the shadows, because I felt that my mother could no longer do anything for me.

The first time they picked me up was in the ninth arrondissement, in the all-night bakery at the foot of rue de Douai. It was already one in the morning. I was standing at one of the tall tables eating a croissant. At that time of night, there are always some strange people in that bakery, and they often come over from the café across the street, the Sans-Souci. Two plainclothes cops came in to do an ID check. I didn't have any identification and they wanted to know how old I was. I decided to tell them the truth. They made me get into the police van alongside a tall blond guy wearing a sheepskin jacket. He seemed to know the cops. Perhaps he was one himself. At one point, he offered me a cigarette, but one of the plainclothes cops stopped him, saying, "She's too young. They're bad for your health." They seemed pretty familiar with each other.

In an office inside the police station, they asked me for my first and last name, my date of birth and address, and they made note of them in a logbook. I explained that my mother worked at the Moulin Rouge. "Well then, we're going to have to give her a call," said one of the two plainclothesmen. The one writing in the logbook gave him the telephone number for the Moulin Rouge. He dialed it, looking me straight in the eye. I felt very embarrassed. He said, "Could I please speak to Madame Geneviève Delanque?" He was still giving me a stern look and I lowered my eyes. And then I heard, "No. No need to disturb her." He hung up. Now he was smiling at me. He had wanted to frighten me. "We'll let it slide this time," he told me, "but next time, I'll have to notify your mother." He got up and we left the police station. The blond fellow in the sheepskin jacket was waiting on the sidewalk. They made me get into the backseat of a car. "Hop in, I'll give you a lift back home," the plainclothes cop told me. Now he was being very casual with me as well. The blond guy in the sheepskin got out of the car at place Blanche, in front of the pharmacy. It felt quite strange to find myself in the backseat of a car driven by a cop. He came to a halt before the front door of our apartment. "Go get some sleep. And miss, no more of that, please." His tone had grown official once again. I think I mumbled a "Thank you, sir." I walked towards the coach entrance, and as I was about to open it, I turned around. He had killed the engine and didn't take his eyes off me for a second, as if he wanted to make sure I actually went into the apartment building. I took a look out of my bedroom window. The car was still parked there. I waited, my forehead glued to the window, curious to see how long he would stay there. I heard the sound of the engine before the car turned the corner and disappeared. I once again experienced the feeling of anxiety that often overwhelmed me at night and was even more intense than fear—the sensation of being completely on my own, without anyone I could turn to. Not my mother, not anyone. I would have liked him to stay all night, on guard in front of the building, all night long and every night like a sentinel, or even better, watching over me like a guardian angel.

Other nights, however, the anxiety dissipated, and I impatiently waited for my mother's departure so I could go out. I went down the stairs with my heart pounding, as if I were going on a date. There was no longer any need to lie to the concierge, to come up with excuses, or to ask permission. To whom? And what for? I wasn't even certain that I would come back to the apartment. Once outside, I didn't take the sidewalk that lay hidden in the shadows, but instead the one that led right past the entrance to the Moulin

Rouge. The lights seemed even more violent than those in the movies at the Mexico. A feeling of intoxication came over me, so subtle and light. I had experienced a similar sensation the night I drank a glass of champagne at the Sans-Souci. I had my whole life ahead of me. How had I turned into such a wallflower, curled up in a little ball? And what was I afraid of? I would meet people. I just had to go into any café.

I knew a girl, a little older than me, named Jeannette Gaul. One night, in the grips of an awful migraine, I had gone into the place Blanche pharmacy to buy some aspirin and a vial of ether. As I went to pay, I realized that I hadn't brought any money. A girl in a raincoat with short blond hair, whose eyes—green eyes—had met mine earlier, stepped forward toward the cash register and paid for me. I was embarrassed, I didn't know how to thank her. I suggested she come back to the apartment with me so I could pay her back. I always kept a little money in my night table. She said, "No, no, next time." She also lived in the neighborhood, but a little farther down. She looked at me, her green eyes smiling. She invited me to go get a drink with her near where she lived, and we ended up in a café—or a bar, rather—on rue de La Rochefoucauld. Not at all the same ambiance as the Condé. The walls were paneled in light wood, as were the bar and the tables, and a sort of stained-glass window looked out onto the street. Subdued lighting. Behind the bar stood a blond woman in her forties that this Jeannette Gaul must have known pretty well judging by the way she casually called her Suzanne. She served us two Pimm's Royales.

"Cheers," Jeannette Gaul said to me. She was still smiling at me and I got the impression her green eyes were probing me, trying to guess what was going on in my head. She asked me, "Do you live around here?"

"Yes. A little farther up."

There were several different zones in the neighborhood, of which I knew all the boundaries, even if they were invisible. As I was intimidated and I didn't really know what to say to her, I added, "Yeah, I live farther up. Here we're only on the lower slopes." She furrowed her brow.

"The lower slopes?" Those two words intrigued her, although she hadn't lost her smile. Was it the effect of the Pimm's? My shyness melted away. I explained to her what I meant by "the lower slopes," an expression I had learned along with all the other schoolchildren in the neighborhood. The lower slopes begin at the Square de la Trinité. They don't stop climbing until you get to the Château des Brouillards and Saint-Vincent Cemetery, and then they dip back down towards the borderlands past Clignancourt, way up north.

"Aren't you just full of information," she said to me. Her smile grew ironic. She seemed to have let her guard down a bit. She ordered two more glasses from Suzanne. I wasn't used to drinking much in the way of alcohol, and one glass was already plenty for me. But I didn't have the nerve to say no. To get it over with more quickly, I drank it in one go. She was still watching me silently.

"Do you go to school?"

I hesitated before I replied. I had always dreamed of being a student, because I found the idea quite glamorous. But that dream had been cut short the day they had rejected my application to the Lycée Jules-Ferry. Was it the self-confidence induced by the champagne? I leaned toward her and, perhaps in order to be more convincing, I brought my face closer to hers.

"Yes, I'm a student."

That first time, I hadn't noticed the other customers around us. Nothing at all like the Condé. If I wasn't worried that I might run into certain ghosts, I would quite happily return to that place one night in order to better understand where I come from. But it pays to be prudent. That said, I'm running the risk of finding it closed down. New ownership. None of it had much of a future.

"A student of what?"

She caught me off guard. The candor of her stare had encouraged me. She certainly couldn't suspect that I was lying.

"Oriental languages."

She seemed impressed. She never asked me subsequently for any details about my studies in Oriental languages, nor for the schedule of the classes, nor the location of the school. She ought to have realized that I wasn't attending any such school. But I believe that for her—and for me as well—it was in some way a title of nobility that I bore, the sort that is inherited without one having to do anything. She introduced me as "the student" to all the regulars in the bar on rue de La Rochefoucauld, and perhaps some of them there still remember me that way.

That night she accompanied me all the way home. In turn, I had wanted to know what she did with her life. She told me that she had been a dancer, but that she'd had to give up that line of work because of an injury. A ballet dancer? No, not exactly, although she had been classically trained. Looking back, I'm left with a question that never would have occurred to me at the time: Had she been a dancer as much as I had been a student? We were following rue Fontaine towards place Blanche. She explained to me that "for the time being" she was a "business partner" of Suzanne's, one of her oldest friends, sort of her "big sister." The two of them ran the spot she had taken me to that evening, which was also a restaurant.

She asked me if I lived alone. Yes, alone with my mother. She wanted to know what my mother did for a living. I didn't speak the words "Moulin Rouge." Dryly, I replied, "Certified accountant." After all, my mother could have been a certified accountant. She was certainly serious enough and had the discretion.

We parted company in front of the coach entrance. It was without the slightest trace of lightheartedness that I returned to that apartment each night. I knew that sooner or later I would leave it for good. I was counting a great deal on the people I would eventually meet, which would put an end to my loneliness. This girl was my first encounter and perhaps she would help me take flight on my own.

"See you tomorrow?" She seemed surprised by my question. I had blurted it out far too abruptly, without managing to conceal my nervousness.

"Of course. Whenever you like."

She shot me another one of her tender, ironic smiles, the same one she had given me earlier when I had explained what I meant by "the lower slopes."

There are holes in my memory. Or rather, certain details are out of order in my mind. For the past five years I have avoided thinking about all of this. And it was enough for the taxi to climb that street and for me to rediscover those illuminated signs: Aux Noctambules, Aux Pierrots ... I no longer remember the name of the place on rue de La Rochefoucauld. The Rouge Cloître? Chez Dante? The Canter? Yes, the Canter. None of the customers of the Condé would have ever patronized the Canter. There are certain invisible boundaries in our lives. And yet, the first few times I went to the Condé, I had been quite surprised to recognize one of the customers I had seen at the Canter: Maurice Raphaël, the one whom everyone called the Jaguar. Never in a million years would I have guessed that this man was a writer. Nothing set him apart from those who played cards and other games in the bar's small back room, behind the wrought-iron gate. I recognized him. I hadn't felt that my face was familiar to him. So much the better. What a relief.

I never really understood what Jeannette Gaul's role was at the Canter. Sometimes she took orders and waited on the customers. She sat with them at the tables. She knew most of them. She introduced me to a tall dark-haired man with a Mediterranean look to him, very well dressed, who gave the impression of being well-educated. A certain Accad, the son of a doctor in the neighborhood. He was always accompanied by two friends, Godinger and Mario Bay. Sometimes, they played cards and other games with the older men in the little back room. This would often go on until five in the morning. One of the cardplayers was apparently the Canter's actual owner. A man in his fifties with short gray hair, also very well dressed, a grim-looking man whom Jeannette told me was a "former lawyer." I remember his name: Mocellini. Once in a while he would get up and join Suzanne behind the bar. Some nights he would stand in for her and serve the drinks himself, just as if he were at home in his own apartment and all of the customers were his guests. He called Jeannette "my dear" or "Crossbones" without my ever understanding why, and the first few times I went to the Canter he looked me over with a fair amount of suspicion. One night, he asked me how old I was. I did my best to make myself look older and said, "Twenty-one years old." He continued to observe me with a frown, he didn't believe me. "You're sure you're twenty-one?" I was growing more and more embarrassed and was nearly ready to tell him my real age, but all of the severity abruptly left his face. He smiled at me and shrugged his shoulders. "Well then, twenty-one years old it is."

Jeannette had a thing for Mario Bay. He wore tinted glasses, but not out of affectation. Light hurt his eyes. He had very delicate hands. At first, Jeannette had taken him for a pianist, one of those, she told me, who perform at Salle Gaveau or the Pleyel. He was around thirty, as were Accad and Godinger. But if he wasn't a pianist, what was it that he did for a living? He and Accad were very tight with Mocellini. According to Jeannette, they had worked for Mocellini when he was still a lawyer. They had worked for him ever since. Doing what? Various business ventures, she told me. But what did that actually mean, "business ventures"? At the Canter, they would often invite us to join them at their table, and Jeannette let on that Accad had a crush on me. Right from the start I got the feeling that she wanted me to get together with him, perhaps in order to strengthen her relationship with Mario Bay. If anything, I had the impression that it was Godinger who had taken a liking to me. He was as dark as Accad, but taller. Jeannette didn't know him as well as the other two. Apparently he had a lot of money and a car that he always parked in front of the Canter. He lived in the hotel upstairs and often traveled to Belgium.

Black holes. As well as details that randomly pop into my head, details as precise as they are insignificant. He lived in the hotel upstairs and he often traveled to Belgium. The other evening, I repeated that stupid sentence over and over as if it were the refrain of a lullaby that you might sing softly in the dark to calm yourself. And why did Mocellini call Jeannette "Crossbones"? Details that conceal other details, much more painful ones. I remember the afternoon a few years later that Jeannette came to visit me in Neuilly. It was a couple of weeks after I married Jean-Pierre Choureau. I never learned to call him anything but Jean-Pierre Choureau, likely because he was older than I was and because he too addressed me so formally. She rang three times as I had requested. For a brief moment, I had the impulse not to answer the door, but that was idiotic, she knew my phone number and address. She came in, sliding through the crack of the half-opened door, and you would have thought she was creeping stealthily into the apartment to commit a burglary. Once we were in the living room, she took a look around, the white walls, the coffee table, the stack of magazines, the red-shaded lamp, the portrait of Jean-Pierre Choureau's mother above the sofa. She didn't say a word. She shook her head. She wanted to take a look around. She seemed stunned when she saw that Jean-Pierre Choureau and I slept in separate rooms. We stretched out on the bed in my bedroom.

"So does he come from a good family?" said Jeannette. And she burst out laughing.

I hadn't seen her since the hotel on rue d'Armaillé. Her laughter made me feel uncomfortable. I was worried she would drag me backwards, back to the days of the Canter. Still, when she had come to visit me in rue d'Armaillé the year before, she had informed me that she no longer had anything to do with the others.

"Such a little girl's room."

Atop the chest of drawers, a picture of Jean-Pierre Choureau in a wine-red leather frame.

"He's pretty handsome. So what's with the separate rooms?"

She once again stretched out on the bed beside me. Then I told her I would prefer to see her anywhere but there. I was worried that she would feel awkward around Jean-Pierre Choureau. And also, we wouldn't be able to speak freely, just the two of us.

"Are you worried I'll bring the others when I come to see you?"

She laughed, but her laughter was less frank than earlier. She was right, I was afraid, even in Neuilly, to run into Accad. I was amazed he hadn't caught wind of me when I was living in the hotels on rue d'Armaillé and then rue de l'Étoile.

"Don't worry. They left Paris a long time ago. They're in Morocco."

She was softly stroking my forehead, as if she wanted to soothe me.

"I'd imagine you haven't told your husband about the parties at Cabassud."

There was no sarcasm in her tone as she spoke. On the contrary, I was touched by the sadness in her voice. It had been her friend Mario Bay, the guy with the tinted glasses and the pianist's hands, who had referred to them as "parties," those nights when he and Accad took us to spend the night at Cabassud, a country home not far from Paris.

"It's so calm here. It's nothing like it was at Cabassud. You remember those nights?"

Details that made me want to squeeze my eyes shut, like

a light that was too bright. And yet, the other night, when we had parted company with Guy de Vere's friends and I was returning from Montmartre with Roland, I kept my eyes wide open. Everything was more distinct, crisp, and clear, an intense light dazzled me and I gradually grew used to it. One night at the Canter, I found myself engulfed by that same light as I sat at a table with Jeannette, by the entrance. Everyone had left except for Mocellini and the others, who were playing cards in the room at the back, behind the gate. My mother would have arrived home hours ago. I wondered if she was worried by my absence. I almost missed the night she had come to pick me up at the Grandes-Carrières police station. It dawned on me that from that point on, she would no longer be able to come and find me. I was too far away. I tried to withstand a wave of anxiety that swept over me, preventing me from being able to breathe. Jeannette brought her face up to mine.

"You're really pale. Aren't you feeling well?"

I wanted to give her a smile to reassure her, but I felt myself grimace instead.

"No. It's nothing."

Ever since I began sneaking out of the apartment at night, I had brief panic attacks, or rather "low blood pressure," as the pharmacist at place Blanche had put it one night when I tried to explain to him what I had been experiencing. But each time a word came out, it seemed either false or meaningless. Better to keep quiet. A feeling of emptiness would come over me in the street. The first time it was in front of the tobacconist's, just past the Cyrano. The street was full of people but that didn't reassure me. I felt as if I were going to faint right there on the spot, and they would just keep on walking straight ahead without paying me any mind at all. Low blood pressure. A power outage. I had to make an internal effort to reset the breaker. That night, I had gone into the tobacconist's and asked for stamps, postcards, a ballpoint pen, and a pack of cigarettes. I sat down at the counter. I took out a postcard and began to write. "Have a little patience. I think things are going to get better." I lit a cigarette and affixed a stamp to the card. But to whom should I address it? I would have liked to write a few words on each one of the cards, reassuring words: "The weather here is beautiful, my vacation is going great. I hope all is well with you too. See you soon. Hugs and kisses." I'm sitting on the patio of a café overlooking the sea, very early in the morning. And I'm writing post-cards to all my friends.

"How are you feeling? Any better?" Jeannette asked me. Her face was even closer to mine. "You want to go out and get some fresh air?"

The street had never seemed that deserted and silent. It was lit by streetlights left over from another era. And to think that climbing the slope was all it would take to rejoin the Saturday-night crowds a few hundred yards farther up, the neon signs promising "The Most Beautiful Nudes in the World," the tourist buses parked in front of the Moulin Rouge. I was scared of all that agitation. I said to Jeannette, "We could stay at mid-slope."

We walked as far as where the lights began, the intersection at the end of rue Notre-Dame-de-Lorette. But there we made a U-turn and descended the hill the same way we had come. I felt more and more relieved as I walked back down the shady side of the slope. I just needed to let myself go. Jeannette held me tightly by the arm. We had nearly arrived at the bottom of the slope, where the street met rue de la Tour-des-Dames. She said to me, "What would you say to us having a little snow?"

I didn't really understand what she meant by that, but the word "snow" caught me off guard. I got the feeling that it would start to fall at any moment and would render the silence that surrounded us even more intense. We would hear nothing but the crunching of our steps in the snow. A clock sounded out somewhere nearby, and, I'm not sure why, I thought it was signaling the start of midnight mass. Jeannette was guiding me. I let myself be carried along. We were following rue d'Aumale, whose every building was shrouded in darkness. It was almost as if they formed a single black wall on either side that spanned from one end of the street to the other.

"Come on into my flat, we'll have ourselves a little snow."

Once we arrived, I would ask her what she meant by "having a little snow." It seemed even colder because of the dark façades. Was I only dreaming when I heard our footsteps echo so distinctly?

Since that day, I have often followed that same route, both with her and alone. I would go and find her in her room during the day, or sometimes I would spend the night there when we stayed too late at the Canter. She lived in a hotel on rue Laferrière, a street located in the lower slopes zone that forms a semicircle where you feel isolated from everything else. An elevator with a wire-mesh door. It climbed very slowly. She lived on the last floor, all the way at the top. Maybe the elevator wouldn't stop. She whispered in my ear, "You'll see, it's going to be great, we'll have ourselves a little snow."

Her hands were trembling. In the dim light of the hallway, she was so nervous that she couldn't manage to insert the key into the keyhole.

"Go ahead, you try. I can't seem to do it."

Her voice grew increasingly unsteady. She had dropped the key. I bent down to grope around for it in the dark. I managed to slide it into the lock. The light was on, a yellow light cast by a ceiling fixture. The bed was unmade, the curtains drawn. She sat down on the edge of the bed and fumbled in the drawer of the nightstand. She withdrew a small metal box. She told me to inhale the white powder she called "snow." After a moment, I began to feel fresh and light. I was certain the anxiety and the feeling of emptiness that often came over me in the street would never return. Ever since the pharmacist at place Blanche had spoken to me about low blood pressure, I had believed that I needed to harden myself, struggle against myself, strive to control myself. Nothing to be done, life had been tough love thus far. Sink or swim. If I fell, everyone else would just keep on walking down the boulevard de Clichy. There was no reason to have any illusions about it. But from now on, things were going to be different. The streets and boundaries of the neighborhood suddenly seemed far too narrow.

A book and stationery shop on the boulevard de Clichy stayed open until one in the morning. Mattei. A lone name stenciled on the front window. The owner's name? I never got up the nerve to ask the brown-haired man with the mustache and the Prince of Wales check suit jacket who was always sitting there reading behind the desk. Customers continually interrupted his reading to buy postcards or a pad of paper. At the time of night I usually went in, there were rarely any customers other than the occasional person coming out of Minuit Chansons next door. Most of the time, he and I were alone in the bookshop. The same books were always on display in the front window, books I soon realized were science fiction novels. He had suggested that I read them. I remember a few of the titles: *Pebble in the Sky*, *Stowaway to Mars*, *Vandals of the Void*. I've only held on to one of them: *The Dreaming Jewels*.

The used books devoted to astronomy were filed on the right-hand side, on the shelves nearest the window. I had come across one with a torn-up orange cover: *Journey into Infinity*. That one I still have. The Saturday night I had intended to buy it, I was the only customer in the store and I could scarcely hear the din of the boulevard. A few neon signs could be seen through the window, including the blue and white of "The Most Beautiful Nudes in the World," but they seemed so very far off. I wasn't bold enough to disturb the man as he read, sitting there, his head down. I stood there in silence the better part of ten minutes before he turned his head my way. I held the book out to him. He smiled. "Very good, this one. Very good. *Journey into Infinity*." I began to get out the money to pay for the book, but he raised his hand. "No, no. This one's on me. And I hope you have a lovely journey."

Yes, that bookstore wasn't only a refuge; it was also a step in my life. I would often stay there until closing time. There was a chair next to the shelves, or rather a tall step stool where I would sit as I leafed through different books. I wasn't sure that he was even aware of my presence. After a few days, without looking up from his reading, he would speak to me, always the same sentence: "So have you found your happiness?" Much later, someone informed me with great certainty that the one thing we cannot remember is the tone of a voice. And yet even now, during my bouts of insomnia, I often hear that voice and its Parisian accent—the accent of the slopes—asking me, "So have you found your happiness?" And that phrase has lost none of its kindness or mystery.

Late at night, stepping back out of the bookstore, I was shocked to once again find myself on the boulevard de Clichy. I didn't really feel like going down to the Canter. My steps led me up instead. I now felt a great deal of pleasure climbing the slopes or the stairs. I counted each step. Once I had counted to thirty, I knew I was home free. Much later, Guy de Vere made me read *Lost Horizon*, a story about some people climbing the mountains of Tibet in search of the monastery of Shangri-La to learn great wisdom and the meaning of life. But it's not worth the trouble going so far. I thought back on my nighttime walks. For me, Montmartre was Tibet. The slope of rue Caulaincourt was plenty for me. Up there, in front of the Château des Brouillards, I could truly breathe for the first time in my life. One day, at dawn, I snuck away from the Canter, having spent the night there with Jeannette. We were waiting for Accad and Mario Bay, who wanted to take us to Cabassud along with Godinger and another girl. I was suffocating. I came up with an excuse to step out for some fresh air. I started running. At place Blanche, all of the neon signs were dark, even that of the Moulin Rouge. I allowed myself to succumb to an intense feeling of intoxication that neither alcohol nor snow had ever given me. I climbed the slope as far as the Château des Brouillards. I had made up my mind never to see the bunch at the Canter again. Later I revisited that same intoxication every time I broke off all ties with someone. I was never really myself when I wasn't running away.

My only happy memories are memories of flight and escape. But life always regained the upper hand. Once I reached the allée des Brouillards, I felt certain that someone had asked me to meet them up there and that it would be a new beginning for me. There is a street a little farther up that I'd like to revisit one of these days. I was following it that morning. That's where I was supposed to meet someone. But I didn't know the number of the building. Didn't matter, I was waiting for a sign that would let me know. At the end of the street ahead of me was wide-open sky, as if it led up to the edge of a cliff. I advanced with that feeling of lightness that can sometimes come to you in a dream. You no longer fear a thing in the world, potential dangers seem laughable. If something goes really wrong, you just need to wake yourself up. You're invincible. I walked on, impatient to reach the end where there was nothing but blue sky and the void. What word would have best described my state of mind? Intoxication? Ecstasy? Rapture? In any case, that road was familiar to me. I felt as if I had walked it before. Soon I would reach the cliff's edge and I would throw myself into the void. What happiness it would be to float through the air and finally know the feeling of weightlessness I had been searching for my whole life. I can still remember that morning with such clarity, that street and that sky at its end.

And then life went on, with its ups and downs. One dismal day, feeling particularly down, as I flipped through the book Guy de Vere had lent me, *Louise, Sister of the Void*, I used a ballpoint pen to replace her name on the cover with my own: *Jacqueline, Sister of the Void*.

THAT NIGHT, it was as if we were at a table-turning séance. We were gathered in Guy de Vere's office, and he had
turned off the lamp. Or perhaps it was simply a power outage. We listened to his voice in the darkness. He was recit-
ing a text that he otherwise would have read under the
light. Well no, I'm not being fair, Guy de Vere would have
been shocked to hear me mention his name in the same
breath as "table-turning" and "séance." He deserved better
than that. He would have said to me, in a slightly chiding
tone, "Honestly, Roland."

He lit the candles of a candelabrum on the mantel then
took his seat behind the desk. We occupied the chairs facing him, that girl, me, and a couple in their early forties
whom I was meeting for the first time, both of them me-
ticulously dressed and rather bourgeois-looking.

I turned my head toward her and our eyes met. Guy de
Vere was still talking, his chest leaned forward slightly but
still naturally, almost as if he was having a casual conversation. At each one of his lectures, he read to us from a text of
which he later provided photocopies. I still have the hand-
out from that night. I had a reference point. She had given
me her phone number and I had written it on the bottom
of the page with a red ballpoint pen.

"Maximum concentration is best reached lying down,

the eyes closed. At the first sign of an external manifestation, dispersion and diffusion will commence. Upright, the legs eliminate a portion of the required strength. Open eyes diminish concentration levels."

It was all I could do to hold in a fit of laughter, and I remember it with certainty because that was the first time it had happened to me there. But the candlelight lent the reading far too much solemnity. My eyes often met those of the girl. Apparently she didn't feel like laughing. Quite the opposite. She seemed very respectful, even worried that she might not understand the meaning of the words. She ended up passing that gravity on to me. I was almost ashamed of my initial reaction. I hardly dared think of the scene I would have caused if I had burst out laughing. And in her gaze, I thought I could see some sort of a cry for help, a question. Am I worthy of being among you? Guy de Vere had folded his hands. His voice had grown even more resolute and he was looking fixedly at her as if she were the only one he was addressing. It petrified her. Perhaps she was afraid he would ask her an unexpected question, something along the lines of "And you, I'd love to hear your opinion on this."

The lights came back on. We lingered in the office a short while longer, which was unusual. The lectures always took place in the living room and gathered together about a dozen people. That evening we were but four, and most likely de Vere had preferred to receive us in his office because of our small number. And the whole thing had been arranged thanks to a simple time and place, without the invitation that was customarily delivered to your home or that you might be given if you were a regular at the Vega bookstore. Like some of the photocopied texts, I've kept a few of those invitations, and yesterday I came across one of them.

Dearest Roland,

Guy de Vere would be delighted to receive you Thursday, January 16th, at 8 p.m.

5 Lowendal Square (15th)

2nd building on the left

4th floor, left door

The white bristol board card, always of the same size and with the same filigreed lettering, could have been announcing a social gathering, a cocktail party, or a birthday.

That evening he accompanied us back down to the door of the apartment. Guy de Vere and the first-time couple all had at least twenty years on us. As the elevator was too small for four people, she and I took the stairs.

A private street lined by identical buildings with beige and brick façades. Same wrought-iron doors under the same old-fashioned streetlights. Same rows of windows. Once through the gate, we found the square at rue Alexandre Cabanel before us. I wanted to write that name down, because that was where our paths first crossed. We lingered a moment in the middle of the square, trying to think of something to say. I was the one to break the silence.

"Do you live in the neighborhood?"

"No, over by Étoile."

I was looking for an excuse not to leave her right away. "We could walk partway together."

We walked under the viaduct, along boulevard de Grenelle. She had suggested we follow the stretch of the Métro that runs above ground towards Étoile. If she got tired, she could always take the Métro the rest of the way. It must have been a Sunday night or a holiday. There was no traffic, all of the cafés were closed. In any case, as I remember it, that night we were in a deserted city. Our having met, when I think about it now, seems like the meeting of two people who were completely without moorings in life. I think that we were both alone in the world.

"Have you known Guy de Vere long?" I asked her.

"No, I just met him at the beginning of the year, through a friend. And you?"

"Through the Vega bookstore."

She wasn't familiar with that bookstore, a shop on boulevard Saint-Germain whose windows bore, in blue lettering, the inscription: "Orientalism and Comparative Religion." That was where I first heard Guy de Vere speak. One evening, the bookseller had given me one of the bristol board invitation cards, telling me that I was welcome to attend the lecture. "It's totally for people like you." I would have liked to ask him what he meant by "people like you." He was looking at me with a fair amount of kindness and it didn't necessarily have to be pejorative. He even offered to "put in a good word" for me with this Guy de Vere.

"Is it any good, this Vega bookstore?"

She had asked me the question with a hint of irony in her voice. Although maybe it was her Parisian accent that gave me that impression.

"You can find all sorts of interesting books there. I'll take you sometime."

I wanted to know what sort of books she read and what had drawn her to Guy de Vere's lectures. The first book that de Vere had recommended to her was *Lost Horizon*. She had read it very carefully. She had arrived at the previous lecture before the others, and de Vere had led her into his office. He hunted through the shelves of his library, which occupied two full walls, for another book to lend her. After a moment, as if an idea had suddenly come to him, he had gone over to his desk and taken up a book that lay among the disorderly heaps of folders and letters. He told her, "You can read this one. I'd be very curious to know what you think of it." She had been extremely intimidated. De Vere always spoke to others as if they were as intelligent and as cultivated as he was. How long could that go on? At some point he would realize that we didn't measure up. The book that he had given her that night was called *Louise, Sister of the Void*. No, I wasn't familiar with it. It related the life story of Louise of the Void, a seventeenth-century nun, and included all the letters she had written. She wasn't reading it from front to back, she just opened it at random. Some pages really made an impression on her. Even more so than *Lost Horizon*. Before meeting de Vere, she had read science fiction novels like *The Dreaming Jewels*. And books about astronomy. What a coincidence. I too had a thing for astronomy.

At Bir-Hakeim station, I wondered if she was going to take the Métro or if she wanted to keep walking and cross the Seine. Above our heads, at regular intervals, the clattering of the trains. We stopped on the bridge and continued our conversation.

"I live up by Étoile, too," I told her. "Maybe not too far from your place."

She was hesitating. She seemed to want to tell me something that was bothering her.

"To be honest, I'm married. I live with my husband in Neuilly." You would have thought she was confessing to a crime.

"Have you been married long?"

"No, not very long. Since last April."

We had resumed walking. We reached the middle of the bridge, where the stairs led to the allée des Cygnes below. She entered the stairwell and I followed her. She made her way down the steps confidently, as if she were on her way to meet someone. And she spoke more and more quickly.

"At one point, I was looking for work. I came across an ad. It was for a job as a temp secretary."

Having reached the landing, we followed the allée des Cygnes. On either side, the Seine and the lights of the quays. I got the impression that I was on the promenade deck of a ship run aground in the dead of night.

"At the office, a man gave me work to do. He was nice to me. He was older... After a while, he wanted to get married."

It seemed as if she was trying to justify herself to a childhood friend whom she hadn't heard from in a long time and had run into in the street.

"What about you? Did you want to get married?"

She shrugged her shoulders, as if my question was absurd. All the while, I was waiting for her to say, "Now look, you know me well enough."

After all, I must have known her in a previous life.

"He always told me he wanted what was best for me. It's true... He does want what's best for me. He kind of takes himself for my father."

I got the feeling she was waiting for my opinion. She didn't seem to be in the habit of confiding in people.

"And he never attends the lectures with you?"

"No. He has too much work to do."

She had met de Vere through an old friend of her husband's. This friend had brought de Vere with him to dinner at their place in Neuilly. She shared all of those details with me, her forehead creased, as if she was afraid to forget a single one, even the most trivial.

We had reached the end of the alleyway, opposite the Statue de la Liberté. A bench on the right. I can't remember which one of us took the initiative to sit down, or perhaps we both had the idea at the same time. I asked her if she shouldn't be getting home. This was the third or fourth time she had attended Guy de Vere's lectures, and each time, towards eleven o'clock at night, she found herself at the foot of the stairs leading into Cambronne station. And each time, at the thought of returning to Neuilly, she felt a kind of discouragement. As it stood, she was doomed to keep taking the same line of the Métro home until the end of her days. Transfer at Étoile. Get off at Sablons.

I could feel her shoulder against mine. She told me that after the dinner at which she had met Guy de Vere for the first time, he had invited her to a talk he was giving in a small room over by Odéon. That day, the subject had been "the Great Noon" and "green light." Upon leaving the room, she had wandered the neighborhood. She floated in the limpid green light Guy de Vere had discussed. Evening, five o'clock. There was a lot of traffic on the boulevard and, at Carrefour de l'Odéon, the crowd jostled her as she walked against the tide, not wanting to go down the stairs into the Métro with them. A deserted street led gently up towards the Jardin du Luxembourg. And there, at mid-slope, she had gone into a café below a building on the corner: the Condé. "Do you know the Condé?" She looked at me inquiringly, suddenly seeming more comfortable. No, I wasn't familiar with the Condé. To be honest, I'm not very fond of the Latin Quarter and all of its schools. It reminded me of my childhood, of the dormitory at the boarding school from which I had been expelled, and of the school cafeteria on the corner of rue Dauphine where I ate my meals thanks to a fake student card. I was starving. Ever since that first time, she had often taken refuge at the Condé. It hadn't taken her long to get to know most of the regulars, and in particular two writers: a fellow named Maurice Raphaël and an Arthur Adamov. Had I heard of them? Sure. I knew who Adamov was. I had even seen him around, over by Saint-Julien-le-Pauvre. A worried look. I would go so far as to say terrified. He walked around wearing sandals on his bare feet. She hadn't read any of Adamov's books. At the Condé, he would occasionally ask her to walk him back to his hotel because he was afraid to walk alone at night. Having become a regular at the Condé, the others had given her a nickname. Her real name was Jacqueline, but they called her Louki. If I wanted, she would introduce me to Adamov and the others. And to Jimmy Campbell, an English singer. And to a Tunisian friend of hers, Ali Cherif. We could meet up at the Condé during the day. She also sometimes went at night when her husband was out. He often returned from work quite late. She looked up at me, and after a moment's hesitation, she told me that each time, she found it a little more difficult to go back to her husband in Neuilly. She seemed troubled and said no more.

Time for the last Métro. We were alone in the car. Before making the transfer at Étoile, she gave me her phone number.

Still to this day, some evenings I hear a voice calling me by name in the street. A somewhat husky voice. It drags a bit around certain syllables, and I recognize it immediately: It's Louki's voice. I turn around, but there's nobody there. Not only in the evenings but during that sluggish part of those summer afternoons when you're no longer even sure what year it is. All will be as it was before. The same days, the same nights, the same places, the same encounters. The Eternal Return.

I often hear that voice in my dreams. It's all so precise—right down to the smallest detail—that I wonder, upon waking, how it could even be possible. The other night, I dreamed I was leaving Guy de Vere's building, at the same time of night it had been when Louki and I left that first time. I looked at my watch. Eleven o'clock at night. There was ivy climbing along one of the ground-floor windows. I passed through the metal gate and I was crossing Cambronne Square towards the above-ground Métro when I heard Louki's voice. She was calling to me: "Roland..." Twice. I could feel the irony in her voice. She had made fun of my name at first, a name that wasn't even my real name. I had chosen it to simplify matters, an all-purpose, everyday name, one that could also serve as a last name. It was quite practical, Roland. And above all, so very French. My real name was too exotic. In those days, I was trying to avoid attracting attention. "Roland..." I turned around. No one. I was in the middle of the square, just like that first time when we hadn't known what to say to each other. When I awoke, I decided to go to where Guy de Vere had lived to see if there really was ivy along the ground-floor window. I took the Métro to Cambronne. It was the line Louki had taken when she was still going home to her husband in Neuilly. I accompanied her, and we often got off at Argentine station, not far from the hotel where I was living. Those evenings, she might have stayed all night in my room, but she made a final effort and went home to Neuilly. And then finally, one night she did stay with me, near Argentine.

I experienced a strange feeling that morning as I walked through Cambronne Square, because it had always been night when we had gone to see Guy de Vere. I pushed open the gate and told myself that there was no way I would run into him after all this time. No more Vega bookstore on boulevard Saint-Germain and no more Guy de Vere in Paris. And no more Louki. But there, running along the ground-floor window, was the ivy, just as it had been in my dream. That disturbed me. Had the other night really been a dream? I lingered a moment, standing motionless at the window. I was hoping I would hear Louki's voice. She would call out my name once again. No. Nothing. Silence. Yet I had the impression that since those days at Guy de Vere's, no time had passed. Instead it had stood still, frozen into some sort of eternity. I remembered the text I had been trying to write back when I knew Louki. I had called it *On Neutral Zones*. There was a series of transitional zones in Paris, no-man's-lands where we were on the border of everything else, in transit, or even held suspended. Within, we benefited from a certain kind of immunity. I might have called them free zones, but neutral zones was more precise. One evening at the Condé, I had asked Maurice Raphaël his opinion, knowing that he was a writer. He shrugged his shoulders and shot me a sardonic smile. "That's for you to figure out, my friend. I don't really understand where you're trying to go with this. I'd say stick with 'neutral' and leave it at that." Cambronne Square, as well as the neighborhood that lay between Ségur and Dupleix, and all of those streets that led to the footbridges of the above-ground Métro, they all belonged to a neutral zone, and it wasn't by chance that I had met Louki there.

I've long since lost that text. Five pages that I had typed on a typewriter lent to me by Zacharias, a customer at the Condé. On the dedication page, I had written, "For Louki of the Neutral Zones." I don't know what she thought of my work. I don't think she had read it all the way through. It was a somewhat off-putting text, a compiled list of the names of the streets, arrondissement by arrondissement, that demarcated the neutral zones. Sometimes a block of houses, sometimes a much larger area. Upon reading the dedication one afternoon at the Condé, she said to me, "You know, Roland, we could go and live a week in each one of these areas you're talking about."

Rue d'Argentine, where I rented a hotel room, was definitely in one of the neutral zones. Who would have been able to find me there? The people I saw there, few and far between, must have been considered dead as far as the state was concerned. One day while flipping through a newspaper, under the heading "Legal Notices," I came across a short entry with the title "Declaration of Absence." Someone named Tarride had never returned home and no one had heard from him in thirty years, so the district court had declared him an "absentee." I had shown the article to Louki. We were in my room on rue d'Argentine. I told her that I was certain the guy lived on my street, along with dozens of others who had also been declared "absentees." Incidentally, the buildings neighboring my hotel all bore the inscription "furnished apartments." Ports of call where no one was asked for identification and where hiding out was easily done. That day, we celebrated La Houpa's birthday with the others at the Condé. They poured us plenty to drink. Back in my room afterwards, we were a little tipsy. I opened the window. At the top of my lungs, I called out, "Tarride! Tarride! . . ." The street was deserted and the name resonated strangely. I even had the impression that it echoed around the neighborhood. Louki came and stood beside me, and she too yelled out, "Tarride! Tarride! . . ." A childish joke that made us laugh. But I ended up believing that this man would show himself and we would resurrect all of the absentees who haunted my street. After a while, the hotel's night watchman came and knocked at our door. With a voice from beyond the grave, he said, "A little silence, if you please." We heard him go back down the stairs with a heavy step. After that, I became convinced that he too was an absentee, just like Tarride, and that the two of them were hiding out in the furnished apartments of rue d'Argentine.

I thought about it every time I went down the street on my way back to my room. Louki had told me that before she married, she had also lived in several different hotels in the area, the first a little farther north, on rue d'Armaillé, then on rue de l'Étoile. In those days, we must have passed on the street without ever noticing each other.

I remember the night she decided she wouldn't go home to her husband anymore. At the Condé that day, she had introduced me to Adamov and Ali Cherif. I was hauling around the typewriter that Zacharias had lent me. I wanted to start *On Neutral Zones*.

I placed the typewriter on the small pitch-pine table in my room. I already had the opening sentence in my mind:

"Neutral zones have at least one advantage: They are only a starting point and we always leave them sooner or later." I was aware that once I sat down in front of the typewriter, everything would be much less straightforward. I would likely end up crossing out that first sentence. And the following one. And yet I found myself full of courage and resolve.

She was expected back in Neuilly for dinner, but at eight o'clock she was still stretched out on the bed. She didn't even switch on the bedside lamp. Eventually I let her know it was time.

"Time to what?"

From the tone of her voice, I understood that she would never again take the Métro out to Sablons. A long silence passed between us. I sat down in front of the typewriter and tapped my fingers lightly on the keys.

"We could go to the movies," she said to me. "That would kill some time."

All we needed to do was cross to the other side of avenue de la Grande-Armée and the Studio Obligado cinema was right there. That evening, I don't think either of us paid the least bit of attention to the film. I don't remember there being many spectators in the theater. The odd person that a district court had declared "absentee"? And what about us? Who were we? I turned and looked at her now and again. She wasn't watching the screen, her head was down and she seemed lost in thought. I was worried she would get up and go back to Neuilly. But no, she stayed until the end of the film.

Once we had left Studio Obligado, she seemed relieved. She told me that it was already too late for her to go back to her husband's place. He had invited a few of his friends out for dinner. There, end of story. There wouldn't be any more dinners in Neuilly, not ever again.

We didn't go back to my room right away. We spent a long time wandering around that neutral zone where we had both taken refuge at different times. She wanted to show me the hotels where she had lived, on rue d'Armaillé and rue de l'Étoile. I'm trying to recall what she said to me that night. It was all rather confused. Nothing but snippets. And it's too late to find the details I'm missing now, or those that I've somehow forgotten. Quite young, she had left her mother and the neighborhood they lived in together. Her mother was dead. She still had a friend from those days that she saw from time to time, a girl named Jeannette Gaul. On two or three occasions we had dinner with Jeannette Gaul on rue d'Argentine, in the run-down restaurant next to my hotel. A blonde with green eyes. Louki told me that people called her Crossbones because of her gaunt face, which stood out in contrast to her generous curves. Later on, Jeannette Gaul would visit her at the hotel on rue Cels, and I ought to have raised an eyebrow the day I walked in on them in her room and the pungent smell of ether was in the air. And then one breezy, sunny day on the quays, across from Notre-Dame, I was browsing through the books in the used-book stalls as I waited for the two of them. Jeannette Gaul had said that she needed to meet someone on rue des Grands-Degrés, someone who was bringing her "a little snow." The word "snow" made her grin, considering it was the middle of July. In one of the booksellers' green bins, I came across a pocket book entitled *The Beautiful Summer*. Yes, it was a beautiful summer, because to me it seemed endless. And I spotted them, all of a sudden, on the quay's other sidewalk, coming from the direction of rue des Grands-Degrés. Louki waved at me. They were walking towards me through the sunshine and the silence. I often see them that way in my dreams, the two of them, down by Saint-Julien-le-Pauvre. I think I was happy that afternoon.

I didn't understand why they called Jeannette Gaul "Crossbones." Because of her high cheekbones and slanted eyes? And yet nothing about her face evoked death. In those days, she was still in that period of her life when youth is more resilient than all else. Nothing—not nights of insomnia, not snow, as she put it—left the slightest mark on her. But for how long? I should have been more wary of her. Louki didn't take her along to the Condé, nor to Guy de Vere's lectures, as if that girl was her dark little secret. I only ever heard them speak of their mutual past in my presence one time, and only cryptically. I got the feeling they had a number of shared secrets. One day as Louki and I stepped out of the Métro at Mabillon—a November day, around six o'clock in the evening, night had already fallen—she recognized someone seated at a table in the large front window of La Pergola. She cringed slightly. A man of about fifty with a stern face and slicked brown hair. He was nearly facing our direction and could have easily seen us as well. But I think he was talking to someone beside him. She took me by the arm and led me to the other side of rue du Four. She told me that she had known the guy a few years earlier, through Jeannette Gaul, and that he ran a restaurant in the ninth arrondissement. She hadn't ever expected to run into him here on the Rive Gauche. She seemed quite anxious. She had used the words "Rive Gauche" as if the Seine were a dividing line separating two different cities, some sort of iron curtain. And the man at La Pergola had somehow managed to cross over that boundary. His presence there, right in front of Mabillon station, really concerned her. I asked her his name. Mocellini. And why was she avoiding him? She didn't give me a clear answer. Quite simply, the guy dredged up unpleasant memories. When she severed ties with people, it was for good, they were dead to her. If this man was still alive and there was a chance she might run into him, then it might be best to move to another neighborhood.

I tried to reassure her. La Pergola wasn't like the other cafés in the area, and its rather shady clientele wasn't at all in keeping with the neighborhood full of students and bohemians through which we were walking. She had told me that she had known this Mocellini in the ninth arrondissement? Well that was precisely it, La Pergola was pretty much an annex to Pigalle that just happened to be in Saint-Germain-des-Prés without anyone really knowing why. It would suffice to take the other sidewalk and avoid La Pergola. No need to move to another neighborhood.

I ought to have insisted on her telling me more, but I knew more or less how she would respond, if she even responded at all. I had been around plenty of Mocellinis during my childhood and teenage years, more than enough of those people about whom, years later, we are left to wonder what kind of racket they were involved in. Hadn't I seen my own father in the company of that sort of person often enough? I could look into this Mocellini character after all these years. But what good would come of it? I wouldn't learn anything about Louki that I didn't know or hadn't already guessed. Can we really be held responsible for those questionable characters, not at all of our choosing, whose paths crossed ours as we were growing up? Am I responsible for my father and for all of those shadowy figures who spoke to him with hushed voices in hotel hallways or in the back rooms of cafés, who carried around suitcases whose contents I would never know? That evening, after our unpleasant encounter, we continued on down the boulevard Saint-Germain. When we entered the Vega bookstore, she seemed relieved. She had a list of a few titles Guy de Vere had recommended to her. I've held on to that list. He used to give it to everyone who attended his lectures. "There is no need to read them all at the same time," he would say. "Instead, choose a single book and read a page of it each night before you go to sleep."

The Celestial Alter Ego
The Friend of God from the Oberland
The Hymn of the Pearl
The Pillar of Dawn
The Twelve Saviors of the Treasure of Light
The Subtle Organs or Centers
The Secret Rose Garden
The Seventh Valley

Small booklets with pale green covers. At first, in my room on rue d'Argentine, we would read them aloud, she and I taking turns. It was a kind of self-discipline, for when we weren't feeling very motivated. I don't believe we read those publications in the same fashion. She hoped to discover some meaning to life within them, whereas it was the sound of the words and the music of the sentences that captivated me. That evening, at the Vega bookstore, seemed to have forgotten all about this Mocellini and the bad memories he conjured up. Thinking back, I realize that it wasn't only a code of conduct that she sought by reading the pale green booklets and the biography of Louise of the Void. She wanted to escape, to run farther and farther away, to break violently with her everyday life, to finally be able to breathe. And then there were also the panic attacks, from time to time, at the thought that those shadowy figures you had left behind might find you and ask you to account for yourself. It was necessary to hide in order to avoid these blackmailers, hoping that one day you would be beyond their reach, once and for all. Way up there, in the fresh mountain air. Or the salty air of the sea. I understood those feelings all too well. I too still carried the bad memories and the nightmarish figures of my childhood around with me, and I hoped that one day I would finally be able to give the finger to the whole lot of them and move on.

I told her that it was foolish to change sidewalks. I ended up convincing her. From then on, when we got off the Métro at Mabillon, we no longer avoided La Pergola. I even dragged her inside the café one night. We stood at the bar and we waited resolutely for Mocellini. And all the rest of the shadows of the past. When she was with me, she wasn't afraid of anything. No better way to make ghosts dissipate than to look them right in the eye. I suspect she had begun to regain her self-confidence and I doubt that she would even have flinched if Mocellini had turned up. I suggested she use the line I had grown accustomed to using in such situations, saying as firmly as possible, "I'm afraid not, sir. That's not me. I'm sorry, you must be mistaken."

We waited in vain for Mocellini that evening. And we never again saw him behind that window.

That February, the month she stopped going home to her husband, it snowed a great deal, and for us, on rue d'Argentine, it was almost as if we were stranded in a remote Alpine lodge. I was coming to realize that it could be difficult to live in a neutral zone. Honestly, it made sense to move closer to the center. The strangest thing about rue d'Argentine—although I had taken an inventory of several other streets in Paris that were quite similar—was that it didn't correspond to the arrondissement where it was situated. It didn't correspond to anything; it was completely disconnected. With that layer of snow, it opened onto the void on either side. I'll have to try to find the list of streets within Paris that are not only neutral zones but also black holes. Or rather, patches of dark matter, which renders everything invisible and which even withstands ultraviolet light, infrared, and X-rays. Yes, in the long run, we will likely all be swallowed up by the dark matter anyway.

She didn't want to remain in a neighborhood that was so close to where her husband lived. Barely two Métro stations away. She was looking for a hotel on the Rive Gauche, in the vicinity of the Condé or near Guy de Vere's apartment. That way she could make the journey on foot. Personally, I was afraid to return to the other side of the Seine, towards the sixth arrondissement of my youth. So many painful memories . . . But what good is there in talking about it, seeing that these days the sixth only exists for those who run the luxury shops that line its streets and the rich foreigners who have bought up its apartments. Back then, I could still find traces of my childhood there: the dilapidated hotels of rue Dauphine, the Sunday-school hall, the Café Odéon where the odd deserter from an American base did his shady dealings, the dark stairs leading to Vert-Galant, and an inscription on the grimy wall of rue Mazarine that I read each time I made my way to school: WORK IS FOR SUCKERS.

When she rented a room a little to the south of there, down towards Montparnasse, I stayed behind near Étoile. I wanted to avoid running into the ghosts on the Rive Gauche. Other than the Condé and the Vega bookstore, I preferred not to spend too much time in my old neighborhood.

And then there was the question of money. She had sold a fur coat that had most likely been a gift from her husband. All she was left with was a raincoat that was much too light to hold up against the winter. She read the want ads, just as she had done shortly before she was married. And once in a while, she went to see a mechanic in Auteuil, an old friend of her mother's who would help her out. I'm embarrassed to admit the sort of work I did myself in those days. But why hide the truth?

A fellow named Béraud-Bedoin lived in the block of houses in which my hotel was located. At 8, rue de Saïgon, to be exact. A furnished apartment. I ran into him quite often, and I can no longer recall when we first ended up having a conversation. A shifty fellow with wavy hair who was always dressed impeccably and gave off an air of world-weary indifference. One winter afternoon as the snow fell on Paris, I sat across from him at a table in the cafe-restaurant on rue d'Argentine. I admitted to him that I wanted to be a writer when he asked me the usual question: "So, what do you do?" As for Béraud-Bedoin, I never really understood what exactly it was that he did. That afternoon, I accompanied him to his "office"—"just around the way," he told me. Our steps left footprints in the snow. We walked straight ahead until we hit rue Chalgrin. I've since consulted an old directory from that year to see exactly where Béraud-Bedoin "worked." Sometimes you remember certain episodes of your life and you need proof that you haven't dreamed them. Fourteen, rue Chalgrin. Commercial Publishers of France. That must be it. Right now I haven't the courage to go down there and see if I recognize the building. I'm too old. He didn't invite me up to his office that day, but we met the following day, same time, same café. He offered me some work. It consisted of writing several brochures about various companies or organizations for which he was in some capacity the promoter or the advertising agent, brochures that would then be printed by his publishing house. He would pay me five thousand francs. His name would appear on the texts. I was to act as his ghostwriter. He would supply all the information. And that is how I ended up working on a dozen short texts, *The Hot Springs of La Bourboule*, *Tourism on Brittany's Emerald Coast*, *The History of the Hotels and Casinos of Bagnoles-de-l'Orne*, as well as monographs about the Jordaan, Seligmann, Mirabaud, and Demachy banks. Each time I sat down at my writing table, I was worried I would fall asleep out of sheer boredom. But it was simple enough, just a matter of reshaping Béraud-Bedoin's notes. I had been surprised the first time he took me to the head office of Commercial Publishers of France: a single windowless ground-floor room. But at the age I was then, you don't ask too many questions. You just trust in life. After two or three months, all contact with my publisher suddenly ceased. He had only given me half the agreed-upon sum, but it was more than enough for me. Maybe one day—why not tomorrow, if I've got the strength—I should go on a pilgrimage to rue de Saïgon and rue Chalgrin, a neutral zone from which both Béraud-Bedoin and Commercial Publishers of France had evaporated that winter along with the snow. But then again, now that I think about it, I haven't really got the courage. I even wonder if those streets still exist, or if they haven't finally been absorbed by the dark matter once and for all.

I'd just as soon take a walk down the Champs-Élysées some spring evening. They don't really exist anymore, but, at night, they still maintain the illusion. Perhaps along the Champs-Élysées I might hear your voice call to me by name. The day you sold the fur coat and the cabochon emerald, I still had about two thousand francs left from the money I had received from Béraud-Bedoin. We were rich. The future was ours. That evening, you were kind enough to come and join me up by Étoile. It was summertime, the same summer we met on the quays, you and me and Crossbones, the afternoon I saw the two of you walking towards me. We went to the restaurant on the corner of rue François-1er and rue Marbeuf. They had put tables out on the sidewalk. It was still daytime. The traffic had thinned and we could hear the murmur of voices and the sound of footsteps. Around ten o'clock, as we made our way down the Champs-Élysées, I asked myself if night would ever fall, if we might be experiencing the midnight sun they get in Russia and the northernmost countries. We walked without any specific destination, we had the whole night ahead of us. There were still patches of sunlight under the arches of rue de Rivoli. It was the beginning of summer, we were going to be leaving soon. Where to? We didn't know yet. Maybe Majorca or Mexico. Maybe London or Rome. The places no longer mattered in the least, they had all blended together into one. The lone goal of our journey was to go to *the heart of summer*, that place where time stops and the hands of the clock permanently show the same hour: twelve noon.

By the time we reached the Palais-Royal, night had fallen. We spent a little while on the patio of the Ruc-Univers before continuing on our way. A dog followed us all the way from rue de Rivoli to Saint-Paul. Then he entered the church. We weren't feeling at all tired, and Louki told me that she felt like she could walk all night. We were crossing a neutral zone just before Arsenal, a few deserted streets that made us wonder if they were uninhabited. On the second floor of a building, we noticed two large illuminated windows. We sat down on a bench opposite them, and we couldn't help but stare at those windows. It was the red-shaded lamp at the very back of the room that cast that muted light. We could make out a gilt-framed mirror on the left wall. The other walls were bare. I watched for a silhouette to pass behind the windows, but no, there was seemingly no one in that room. We couldn't tell if it was a living room or a bedroom.

"We should ring the doorbell," Louki said to me. "I'm sure someone is expecting us."

The bench was in the center of a kind of island formed by the intersection of two streets. Years later, I was in a taxi heading past Arsenal towards the quays. I asked the driver to stop. I wanted to find that bench and that building. I hoped that the two second-floor windows would still be illuminated after all that time. But I very nearly got lost among the numerous small streets that surrounded the walls of the Célestins barracks. That night, I had told her there was no point in ringing the doorbell. No one would be home. And plus, we were just fine there on that bench. I could even hear a fountain gurgling somewhere nearby.

"Are you sure?" Louki had said. "I don't hear anything."

We were the ones who lived in that apartment. We had forgotten to turn out the light. And we had misplaced the key. The dog from earlier must have been waiting for us. He had fallen asleep in our bedroom and he would remain there, waiting for us until the end of time.

Later that night, we were walking northward, and so as not to drift too far, we had set a goal: place de la République, although we weren't certain we were going the right direction. It didn't really matter, we could always take the Métro back to Argentine if we ended up getting lost. Louki told me she had spent a lot of time in that area when she was younger. Her mother's friend Guy Lavigne had had a garage nearby. Yes, somewhere near République. We kept stopping at every garage, but it was never the right one. She could no longer find her way. The next time she paid a visit to Guy Lavigne out in Auteuil, she would have to ask him the exact address of his old garage, before he too disappeared. It didn't seem important, but it was. Otherwise, it was possible to end up without a single reference point in your life. She remembered that her mother and Guy Lavigne used to take her to the Foire du Trône carnival on the Saturday that followed Easter. They walked there, down a never-ending boulevard that looked much like the one we were following. It had to be the same one. But then we must have been moving away from place de la République. On those Saturdays, she walked with her mother and Guy Lavigne all the way to the edge of the Bois de Vincennes.

It was nearly midnight, and it would be strange to find ourselves at the gates of the zoo. We would be able to make out the elephants in the darkness. But there ahead of us sprawled a brightly lit open space in the middle of which stood a statue. Place de la République. As we drew nearer, music grew louder and louder. A ball? I asked Louki if it was the fourteenth of July. She didn't know any more than I did. For the last while, the days and nights had all been running one into the next for the both of us. The music was coming from a café a little ways from where the boulevard met rue du Grand-Prieuré. A few customers seated on the terrace.

It was too late to catch the last Métro. Just beyond the café, a hotel, its door open. A bare lightbulb illuminated a very steep stairwell with black wooden steps. The night clerk didn't even ask our names. He simply gave us the number of a room on the second floor. "Maybe we could just live here from now on," I said to Louki.

A single bed, but it wasn't too narrow for the two of us. No curtains or shutters on the window. We left it open because of the heat. Below, the music had gone quiet, and we could hear peals of laughter. She whispered in my ear, "You're right. We should just stay here forever."

I felt like we were far from Paris, in a small Mediterranean port. At the same time every morning, we followed the path down to the beach. I still remember the hotel's address: 2, rue du Grand-Prieuré. Hôtel Hivernia. All throughout the bleak years that followed, whenever someone would ask me my address or telephone number, I would say, "You can always write to me at the Hôtel Hivernia, 2, rue Grand-Prieuré. It will be forwarded to me." I really should go and pick up all the letters that have been waiting there for me for such a long time, letters that have gone unanswered. You were right, we should have stayed there forever.

I saw Guy de Vere one last time, quite a few years later. In the street that slopes down toward Odéon, a car came to a halt next to me and I heard someone call me by my former name. I recognized the voice even before I turned around. He leaned his head out the lowered car door window. He smiled at me. He hadn't changed. Except for slightly shorter hair.

It was in July, around five o'clock in the evening. It was hot out. We both took a seat on the hood of the car to talk. I didn't have it in me to tell him that we were only a few yards away from the Condé and the door Louki had always used, the one hidden in the shadows. In any case, that door didn't exist anymore. Facing the street, there was now a window displaying crocodile handbags, boots, even a saddle and riding crops. The Prince de Condé. A leather shop.

"Well, Roland, what have you been doing with yourself?"

It was still the same strong, clear voice, the one that had made the most abstruse texts accessible when he read them to us. I was touched that he remembered me and the name I had gone by in those days. So many people had attended those lectures at Lowendal Square. Some of them only came once, out of curiosity, while others attended religiously. Louki belonged to the latter group. As did I. And yet Guy de Vere hadn't been in search of disciples. He didn't in any way consider himself a guru or a mentor, and he had no interest in exerting any sort of control over others. They were the ones who came to him, without him soliciting them. Sometimes it had seemed to us that he would have preferred to be left alone to dream, but he couldn't refuse those people anything, especially when it came to helping them see more clearly within themselves.

"And how about you, are you back in Paris now?"

De Vere smiled at me and shot me a wry look.

"You haven't changed a bit, Roland. You still answer a question with another question."

He hadn't forgotten that, either. He had often teased me about it. He had told me that if I had been a boxer, I would have been a master of the feint and parry.

"I haven't lived in Paris for quite some time now, Roland. I've been living in Mexico. I ought to give you my address."

The day I had gone to verify whether or not there was ivy on the ground floor of his former building, I had asked the concierge for Guy de Vere's new address, on the slim chance that she had it. She had simply replied, "Gone with no forwarding address." I told him about that pilgrimage to Lowendal Square.

"You're incorrigible, Roland, you and your ivy. You were pretty young back when I knew you, weren't you? How old would you have been?"

"Twenty."

"Well, it seems to me that even at that age, you were off in search of lost ivy. Am I right?"

His gaze never left me and a cloud of sadness passed across it. We were likely thinking the same thing, but I didn't dare mention Louki's name.

"It's strange," I told him. "Back when we used to have

our lectures, I went to this café quite often, although it isn't a café anymore."

And I motioned to the leather shop a few yards away from us, The Prince de Condé.

"Of course," he said to me, "Paris has changed a lot over the last few years."

He studied me, his brows furrowed, as if he were trying to access a distant memory.

"Are you still working on the neutral zones?"

The question came out of nowhere and I didn't understand what he was referring to at first.

"It was pretty interesting, your text on neutral zones."

My God, what a memory. I had forgotten that I made him read that text. One evening after one of the lectures at his place, Louki and I had been the last to leave. I had asked him if he might have a book on the Eternal Return. We were in his office and he hunted through a few of the shelves in his library. He finally found a book with a black and white cover, *Nietzsche's Philosophy of the Eternal Recurrence of the Same*, which he gave to me, and I spent the following several days reading it attentively. The few typed pages about the neutral zones had been in the pocket of my jacket. I wanted to give them to him in order to get his opinion, but I was hesitant. It was only as we were leaving, on the landing outside his door, that I abruptly made up my mind to hand him the envelope I had filled with the scant pages— all without saying a word.

"You were also very interested in astronomy," he said. "By dark matter, in particular."

I never would have dreamed that he would remember that. I was aware that he had always paid close attention to others, but when it was happening, you didn't really notice.

"It's too bad," I told him, "that there isn't a lecture at Lowendal Square tonight, like there used to be ..."

My words seemed to surprise him. He smiled at me.

"And there's your old obsession with the Eternal Return."

By this point we were walking up and down that length of sidewalk, and each time, our path led us past the Prince de Condé leather shop.

"Do you remember the night the power was out at your place and you gave your lecture in the dark?" I asked him.

"No."

"I've got to admit something to you. I was inches away from having a crazy laughing fit that night."

"You should have let it out," he chided me. "Laughter is infectious. We all would have had a laugh in the dark." He looked at his watch. "I've got to get going. I have to pack my suitcases. I'm leaving again tomorrow. And I haven't even had time to find out what you're doing with yourself these days."

He took a day planner from the inside pocket of his jacket and tore a page from it.

"I'm giving you my address in Mexico. You really should come see me."

He had suddenly adopted a peremptory tone, as if he wanted to take me along with him and save me from myself. And from the present.

"And what's more, I'm still giving my lectures over there. Come. I'll be expecting you."

He held out the sheet of paper to me.

"You've got my phone number there as well. This time, let's not lose touch."

Back in the car, he once again leaned his head out the window.

"Tell me . . . I often think of Louki . . . I never understood why . . ."

He was overwhelmed by emotion. This man who always spoke without hesitation, so clearly, he was at a loss for words.

"What I just said is ridiculous. There's nothing to understand. When we really love someone, we've got to accept their role in the mystery. And that's why we love them. Isn't it, Roland?"

He drove off abruptly, most likely to cut short his emotions. And my own. He had time only to say, "See you soon, Roland!"

I was left on my own in front of the Prince de Condé leather shop. I pressed my forehead to the window in an effort to see if any trace whatsoever remained of the café: a section of wall, the rear door that led to the telephone, the spiral staircase that led to Madame Chadly's little apartment. Nothing. Everything was stark and featureless, covered with an orange fabric. And the whole neighborhood was like that. At least there was no longer any reason to worry about running into ghosts. The ghosts themselves were dead. No need for concern on the way out of the Métro at Mabillon. No more La Pergola and no more Mocellini lurking in the window.

I walked with a spring in my step, as if I had arrived in a foreign town on some July evening. I began whistling a Mexican tune, but this fictitious carefree attitude was short-lived. I made my way along the wrought-iron fence that rings the Luxembourg, and the melody from "Ay Jalisco no te rajes" vanished from my lips. A notice was attached to the trunk of one of the great trees whose leaves offer shelter on the way to the entrance to the gardens further along at Saint-Michel. "DANGER. This tree will be cut down soon.

It will be replaced by a new one this coming winter." For a brief second, I thought I was having a bad dream. I stood there, frozen, reading and rereading that death warrant. Someone came over to me and said, "Are you all right, sir?," then he continued on, likely thrown by my blank stare. In this world where I felt more and more like a holdover, the trees were on death row, too. I continued on my way, trying to think of other things, but it was easier said than done. The image of that notice and that tree, condemned to death, was burned into my brain. I tried to picture the faces of the jury and the executioner. I regained my composure. To comfort myself, I pictured Guy de Vere walking along beside me, repeating in his soft voice, "Of course not, Roland, it's just a bad dream. People don't murder trees."

I had passed the entrance gate that led to the gardens and was following the boulevard towards Port-Royal. One night, Louki and I had accompanied a boy of about our age along this stretch, someone we had gotten to know a bit at the Condé. He had pointed out the École des Mines buildings on our right, informing us in a sad voice, as if the admission had been weighing heavily on him, that he went to school there.

"Do you think it's worth the effort?"

I had felt that he was seeking encouragement from us to pull the plug. I had told him, "Of course not, my friend, don't bother with it. Time to get on with your life."

He had turned towards Louki. He was waiting for her advice as well. She had explained to him that ever since she had been refused admission to the Lycée Jules-Ferry, she hadn't put much stock in schools. I think that had managed to convince him. The next day, back at the Condé, he had told us that he was finished with the École des Mines.

She and I would often take that same route on our way back to her hotel. It was a bit of a detour, but we were in the habit of walking. Was it really out of our way? Well no, not when I think about it, it was more like a straight line heading inland. At night, all the way down avenue Denfert-Rochereau, it felt as if we were in a provincial town because of the silence and the doors of the religious hospices that came one after another. The other day, I walked along the plane trees and high walls of the road that cuts Montparnasse Cemetery in two. It was also the way to her hotel. I remember that she preferred to avoid it, which is why we usually took Denfert-Rochereau. But towards the end of those days, we were no longer afraid of anything and found that the road that cut through the cemetery had a certain charm to it at night as we passed beneath its canopy of leaves. There were no cars at that hour, and we never saw a soul. I had forgotten to record it on the list of neutral zones. It was more of a boundary. When we reached the end, we entered a land where we were shielded from everything. Last week, it hadn't been nighttime when I walked there, but rather late afternoon. I hadn't been back since the days we used to walk down that road together, since I would take it on my way to meet you at the hotel. For a moment, I got the feeling that once I passed the cemetery you would be there. Once I arrived, it would be the Eternal Return. The same routine as always to get the key to your room from the front desk. The same steep stairwell. The same white door with its number: 11. The same anticipation. And then the same lips, the same scent, your hair cascading down the same way.

I could still hear what de Vere had said to me about Louki, "I never understood why...When we really love someone, we've got to accept their role in the mystery."

What mystery? I had been certain that we were so alike, she and I, because we could often read each other's minds. We were on the same wavelength. Born the same year and the same month. And yet, believe it or not, there must have been a fundamental difference between us.

No, I can't understand it either. Especially when I remember those final weeks. The month of November, the days growing shorter, the autumn rain, none of it managed to shake our morale. We were even making travel plans. On top of that, a joyful ambiance filled the Condé. I can no longer recall who had introduced Bob Storms among the regular customers, a man who claimed to be a poet and a stage director from Antwerp. Perhaps Adamov? Or Maurice Raphaël? He really made us laugh, that Bob Storms. He had a soft spot for Louki and me. He wanted us to spend the summer in his villa in Majorca. Apparently, he had nothing in the way of financial concerns. Rumor was he collected paintings. You know how people talk. And then people just vanish one day and you realize you didn't know the first thing about them, not even who they really were.

Why is the imposing shadow of Bob Storms suddenly looming so prominently in my mind? In life's most tragic moments, there is often a light note that sounds out of tune with the rest, a court jester, a Bob Storms who passes through and who might have been able to ward off any impending misfortune. He always stood at the bar, as if the wooden chairs might collapse beneath his weight. He was so big that his corpulence wasn't even visible. Always wearing a kind of velvet doublet, the black of which contrasted with his red beard and hair. And a cloak of the same color. The evening we first noticed him, he made his way to our table and looked us over from top to bottom, Louki and I.

Then he smiled, and leaning toward us, he whispered, "Companions in unpleasant times, I wish you the best of nights." When he learned that I could recite a good many poems, he had insisted that we have a contest. The winner would be the one who had the last word. He would recite a line of verse, I would reply with another, and so on. It went on for quite some time. I didn't really deserve any of it. I was more or less illiterate, lacking much in the way of general culture, I just happened to have retained some poetry, not unlike those people who can play any piece of music on the piano and yet don't know the first thing about music theory. Bob Storms had one advantage over me: He also knew the entire repertoire of English, Spanish, and Flemish poetry. Standing at the bar, he defiantly sent forth his challenge:

> *Et que le cheval fit un écart en arrière.*
> *"Donne-lui tout de même à boire," dit mon père.*

or:

> *Como todos los muertos que se olvidan*
> *En un montón de perros apagados*

or again :

> *De burgemeester heeft ons iets misdaan,*
> *Wij leerden, door zijn schuld, het leven haten.*

Sometimes I found him a bit tiresome, but he was a good guy, quite a bit older than we were. I would have loved to hear him talk of his past lives. He always answered my questions evasively. When he felt that too much curiosity was being directed his way, his exuberance melted away immediately, as if he had something to hide or wanted to cover his tracks. He wouldn't respond, and then would finally break the silence with a burst of laughter.

One night Bob Storms hosted a soirée at his place. He invited Louki and me, along with the others: Annet, Don Carlos, Bowing, Zacharias, Mireille, La Houpa, Ali Cherif, and the guy we had convinced to quit the École des Mines. Other guests as well, but I didn't know them. He lived on the Quai d'Anjou in an apartment whose upper floor was an enormous studio. He invited us there for a reading of *Hop Signor!*, a play he wanted to direct. The two of us arrived before the rest, and I was blown away by the candelabra that lit the studio, the Sicilian and Flemish marionettes hung from the crossbeams, the Renaissance mirrors and furniture. Bob Storms was wearing his black velvet doublet. A giant bay window gave onto the Seine. He protectively encircled Louki's shoulders and my own, and he spoke his customary words:

"Companions in unpleasant times
I wish you the best of nights."

Then he took an envelope from his pocket and held it out to me. He explained to us that it contained the keys to his house in Majorca, and that we ought to head there as soon as we were able. And stay until September. He thought we were looking a bit unhealthy. What a strange night. The play was only one act long and the actors read it rather quickly. We were seated around them in a circle. Once in a while, during the reading, on a cue from Bob Storms, we all had to cry out "Hop Signor!" in unison, as if we were part of a chorus. The alcohol flowed freely. As well as other intoxicants. A buffet had been set up in the middle of the large parlor on the lower floor. Bob Storms himself served drinks in elaborate goblets and crystal stemware. More and more people. At one point, Storms had introduced me to a man of about his age, although much smaller than he was, an American writer named James Jones whom he described as "his next-door neighbor." Eventually Louki and I began to wonder what we were doing there among all of those people we didn't know. All of those people who had in some way been mixed up with our early years, people who would never be aware of it and whom we wouldn't even recognize later on.

We slowly slipped towards the exit. We were sure that no one had noticed our departure amidst all the chaos. Yet we had hardly passed the door to the parlor when Bob Storms appeared before us.

"Well then, are you trying to ditch me, children?"

He wore his usual smile, a broad smile that, along with his beard and towering stature, brought to mind a character from the Renaissance or the seventeenth century, Rubens or Buckingham. All the same, a flash of worry was visible in his gaze.

"You weren't too bored, I hope?"

"Of course not," I told him. "*Hop Signor!* was really great."

He once again wrapped his arms around our shoulders, both Louki's and mine, just as he had done in the studio.

"Well then, I hope I'll be seeing you tomorrow."

He led us to the door, still holding us by the shoulders.

"And don't forget, head for Majorca as soon as you're able, to get some fresh air. You need it. I've given you the keys to the house."

On the landing, he took a good, long look at both of us. Then he recited, for my benefit:

"The sky is like the torn midway tent of a poor circus
in a fishing village in Flanders."

We made our way down the stairs, Louki and I, and he lingered, leaning over the banister. He was waiting for me to recite a verse in response to his, as we were in the habit of doing. But I drew a blank.

I feel as if I'm starting to mix up the seasons. A few days after that soirée, I accompanied Louki as she went out to Auteuil. I seem to remember it being summer, or at least one of those winter mornings that are so clear and cold, with sunshine and blue skies. She wanted to pay a visit to Guy Lavigne, the man who had been a friend of her mother's. I had decided that I would prefer to wait for her. We had arranged to meet in an hour, on the corner down the street from his garage. I think we were intending to leave Paris because of the house keys Bob Storms had given us. Sometimes the heart aches at the very thought of things that might have been and never were, but to this very day, I tell myself that the villa in Majorca is still sitting there empty, waiting for us. I was happy that morning. I felt as light as air, a sensation of intoxication. The horizon lay straight out ahead of us, way out there, towards infinity. A garage at the end of a quiet street. I regretted not having gone with Louki to meet this Lavigne. Maybe he would have lent us a car for our trip south.

I saw her exit through the small door of the garage. She waved at me, exactly the same way she had that other time, when I was waiting for her and Jeannette Gaul that summer day on the quays. She's coming towards me with that nonchalant walk of hers, and it's as if she's reduced her speed even more, as if time no longer mattered. She takes me by the arm and we wander the neighborhood. We will live here one day. In fact, this is where we've always lived. We walk down the quaint streets, we cross the deserted roundabout. The village of Auteuil very gently breaks away from Paris. The ocher or beige-colored buildings could easily be on the Côte d'Azur, and those walls, who knows whether they conceal a garden or the edge of a forest. We reached the place de l'Église, in front of the Métro station. And there, I can say it now that I no longer have anything left to lose: I felt, for the first time in my life, what the Eternal Return really was. Up until then, I had struggled to read books on the subject, with the determination proper to an autodidact. It was just before we went down the steps into the Métro at Église-d'Auteuil. Why there, of all places? I haven't the slightest idea, and it doesn't matter anyway. I stood still a moment and I held her arm tightly. We were there, together, in the same place, for all of eternity, and our stroll through Auteuil, we had already taken it during thousands and thousands of other lives. No need to look at my watch. I knew it was noon.

It happened in November. On a Saturday. That morning and afternoon I had stayed in rue d'Argentine to work on the neutral zones. I wanted to flesh out the four pages, to write at least thirty. It would snowball from there and I would be able to reach the hundred-page mark. I was to meet Louki at the Condé at five o'clock. I had decided to leave rue d'Argentine for good during the next few days. I felt that I was finally over the scars of my childhood and teenage years and that going forward, I no longer had any reason to remain hidden in a neutral zone.

I walked as far as the Métro station at Étoile. That was the line we had taken so many times before, Louki and I, to go to Guy de Vere's lectures, the line we had followed on foot that first night. As I crossed the Seine, I noticed that there were a lot of people out walking along the allée des Cygnes. Transfer at La Motte-Picquet-Grenelle.

I got off at Mabillon, and I glanced toward La Pergola, as we always had. Mocellini wasn't sitting in the window.

When I entered the Condé, the hands of the round clock on the back wall showed exactly five o'clock. It was usually pretty dead at that time of day. The tables were empty, with the exception of the one next to the door, which was occupied by Zacharias, Annet, and Jean-Michel. All three of them were giving me strange looks. No one said a word. Zacharias's and Annet's faces were both very pale, likely from the light pouring in through the window. They didn't respond when I said hello. They stared at me with those strange looks on their faces as if I had done something awful. Jean-Michel pursed his lips, and I felt that he wanted to tell me something. A fly landed on the back of Zacharias's hand and he swatted it away with a nervous slap. Then he picked up his drink and downed the entire glass. He got up and walked over toward me. With a flat, expressionless voice, he said, "Louki. She threw herself out the window."

I was afraid I might lose my way. I took Raspail and then

the road that cut through the cemetery. Once I reached its end, I no longer knew whether I should keep walking straight or if I needed to follow rue Froidevaux. I took rue Froidevaux. From that moment forward, there was an absence in my life, a blank space that not only gave me a feeling of emptiness but that I couldn't bear to look at. All of that blank space blinded me with a bright and radiant light. And it will be like that until the very end.

Quite a bit later, at Broussais Hospital, I sat in a waiting room. A man in his fifties with a gray brush cut and a herringbone coat was also waiting on a bench on the other side of the room. Other than the two of us, the room was empty. The nurse had come to tell me that she was dead. The man came over to us as if it concerned him. I thought he must have been Guy Lavigne, the friend of her mother's whom she visited at his garage in Auteuil. I asked him.

"Are you Guy Lavigne?"

He shook his head.

"No, my name is Pierre Caisley."

We left Broussais together. Night had fallen. We walked side by side down rue Didot.

"And I suppose you must be Roland?"

How could he know my name? I had difficulty walking. That blank space, that radiant light before me.

"She didn't leave a note?" I asked him.

"No. Nothing."

He was the one who gave me all the details. She was in the room with a girl named Jeannette Gaul, whom some knew as Crossbones. But how did he know Jeannette's nickname? She had gone out on the balcony. She had put one leg over the railing. The other girl had tried to hold her back by the shirttail of her dressing gown. But it was too late. She had time only to say a few words, as if to give herself courage:

"That's it. Just let yourself go."

TITLES IN SERIES

For a complete list of titles, visit www.nyrb.com or write to:
Catalog Requests, NYRB, 435 Hudson Street, New York, NY 10014

* *Also available as an electronic book.*